Welcome to
December
7
1972

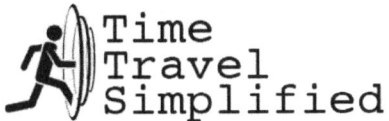

Final Apollo Mission

December 7, 1972

Time Travel Simplified

A Curated Multimedia

Time Travel Experience

Mark Hatala, Ph.D.

Time Travel Press

Final Apollo Mission - December 7, 1972
Time Travel Simplified: A Curated Multimedia Time Travel Experience
by Mark Hatala, Ph.D.

ISBN-13: 978-1-933167-72-5
ISBN-10: 1-933167-72-6

Book Design: Charles Dunbar

The font used in this book is Times New Roman, with headings in Courier

To incorporate this book into your life experience, visit our website at
timetravelsimplified.com

Table of Contents

"The past is a foreign country; they do things differently there."

- L. P. Hartley, *The Go-Between*

Days fly by in a blur, with one day seemingly like the next. But what if you could stop time, and examine one day in depth? Read the news from that day. Enjoy the print media. Watch television. See the commercials.

And what if you revisited that day over and over again - what insights would you take away about that day, and about yourself? That's the purpose of this book, and the promise of time travel. Quite simply, time travel is a "magic well" - the more you draw out of it, the more there is to take.

We often think of time travel as we see it portrayed in science fiction or popular movies like the *Back to the Future* series. In these scenarios, a person steps into a "time machine" (which may or may not be a DeLorean automobile) and vanishes into another time. Once there, the person has to deal with the known "paradoxes" of time travel, such as avoiding altering the past in such a way that it negatively impacts the present (or future). They also have stereotypical views of the time they are travelling to.

That is NOT what this project is about. I have no physical "time machine" for you to step into to visit the past.That's not a problem though. Ironically, you have the time machine with you at all times, and the real paradox of time travel is not that time travel changes the past - it's that it changes you. Who you are. How you see the world. How you see the past and the present, and how you see yourself fitting into the greater human experience.

The ability to use your own critical analysis of what you've experienced in the past and apply it to your own time is the gift of time travel. Not only will you understand the past, you'll understand how we got to this particular present, and most importantly, you'll understand yourself - your hopes, fears, biases, influences, and ways of seeing the world - in an entirely new way. Time travel, at its core, is about human potential and personal growth.

This book examines December 7, 1972. While I physically experienced that day, I cannot say that I understood it. It would be easy to say that this is due to the fact that I was six years old and living in the suburbs of Cleveland, but the fact is that it was a day like any other. The high for the day in Cleveland was 25 and the low was 18, and there was .3 inches of snow that fell, so just a dusting. How many other December days have been exactly like that? Since it was a Thursday, I know it was a school day, and so I can be pretty sure I ate a peanut butter sandwich with an apple for lunch, because that's what I ate EVERY day for lunch when I was six.

My point is that it doesn't matter whether you've experienced a day in "reality" in order to understand it. Even historic events that I was an adult for, such as the attacks of September 11th, I'm sure I would interpret differently now.

Historians often say that when examining a particular historical event, we should forget what we know about it because people at the time didn't have any idea how things were going to turn out. This is an obvious fallacy, because in general, we DO know how things turned out. And what we don't know, we can research or look up online. This is our enormous advantage over people in the past. Call it the "time traveler's edge."

One of the goals of this time travel experience is to make you "fluent" in December 1972. You will understand the major historical issues of the time through the eyes of the people living, writing, and acting in that time. You'll understand the inside jokes and the social trends. What is going to happen in the Women's Liberation Movement? The war in Vietnam? The Space Program? Organized crime? These are the issues which dominated the media conversation of December 1972. Soon you'll see why.

This isn't a history of December 1972. Histories are written by people from a later era to explain an earlier era to people of their own time. Using the methodology developed for Time Travel Simplified, you will see that the person from a later era explaining another era to you is you. You're not a historian. Or even a "time tourist" who visits and leaves.

You're a time traveller. Someone who understands the past because they've lived there.

This book is divided into four sections with research and learning modules throughout.

Setting the Stage is the first section, and the goal is to familiarize you with the zeitgeist ("spirit of the times") of December 1972. Most of the media is in print, and so this section has a large reading component. However, the visual media is also significant, and includes the Apollo 17 prelaunch news coverage from both December 5th and December 6th. Each source has several modules, and so there are 70 modules for this section.

The Day is the second section, and it is all about the media from December 7th 1972. It begins with footage of the launch of Apollo 17 at 12:33AM from Kennedy Space Center in Florida and ends with *The Tonight Show with Johnny Carson* from Burbank, California. So we go geographically from coast to coast! In between is an entire day's worth of programming - game shows, reruns, and primetime shows. Also included are print media from that day, including two different newspapers (the *New York Times* and the *Chicago Tribune*), as well as magazines that came out that day (like *Jet* and *Rolling Stone*). While you should take longer than a day to complete the 60 modules dedicated to December 7th, you will understand that single day better than you do any other. That's time travel - simplified.

Debriefing is the third section, and it is significant in a few important ways. First, it includes the print media which came out right after December 7th, such as the *New York Daily News*, *Life* magazine, and the *New Yorker*. These are invaluable because they teach what the "gatekeepers" of the news media considered to be the important news from that week. Second, it includes retrospectives on the Apollo 17 mission. For example, the documentary *Last Man on the Moon* tells the life story of mission commander Eugene Cernan, who was, like Neil Armstrong, a part of the Gemini and Apollo Programs. In other words, the *Debriefing* covers what the people who lived through the experience considered significant and important from the day after the event to four decades later.

The *Background Research* is the final section, and covers the cognitive science and memory research which explains why you'll remember December 7th 1972 as if you lived through it. Spoiler alert: it's because you did! That's the guarantee of the Time Travel Simplified methodology - it's time travel or it's free! It's not necessary to read this section in order to understand time travel, but it's there (with citations and references) if you're interested.

I want to close this introduction by welcoming you into our Society of Time Travelers. We've all shared a unique experience that we can talk about on the discussion forums at timetravelsimplified.com. Each of us brings a unique perspective to the past, and sharing it with others, especially fellow time travelers, is part of the reward. Thank you for joining me on this journey. Let's get started!

A note on accessing materials online

All of the print and visual media mentioned in this book are available online at timetravelsimplified.com - it's easy to access - just look for "December 7 1972" at the top of the page or click on the picture of the book. That will take you directly to the page with all of the modules.

I think that the material is most conveniently accessed via a tablet, laptop, or desktop computer. An advantage of a tablet is that many people are familiar with reading media or watching video on a tablet. Laptop and desktop computers are also good because the media is scaled to be easily read.

While I realize that many people (especially young people) read everything on their phones, I believe that the amount of material accessible on a phone doesn't lead to the best reading experience. However, that might be my own opinion! The modules are often presented out of order on the "December 7 1972" page when you use a phone to access the material. All the modules are still there, but you might have to hunt around to find the one you want.

Again, no matter how you're accessing the online materials, all of the modules, by number, can be accessed via the "December 7 1972" page.

A note about modules

There are blank spaces (and entire pages) throughout the print version of this book (I'm afraid you'll have to get a notebook if you buy one of the Kindle "sample" versions) for you to write down your thoughts and reactions to the modules. You could type out your answers, but research has shown that recording your notes in the book (or a notebook) in your own handwriting leads to better memory consolidation through a phenomenon called the *generation effect*. Therefore, that's what I recommend, and why I designed the book this way.

This isn't a "textbook" - it's a workbook!

14

Setting the Stage

This first section is dedicated to providing context for December 7th 1972, and so it begins with brief coverage of some of the major events of the 1960's - the Kennedy assassination, the Beatles, and the moon landing achieved by Apollo 11. Is it a coincidence that I'm also writing Time Travel Simplified books about these particular dates (November 22, 1963, February 9, 1964, July 20, 1969) and am trying to garner interest in these books? Perhaps.

We then move directly into late 1972, with a juxtaposition of *Ms.* magazine and *Cosmopolitan*, which present two very different approaches to the Women's Liberation Movement.

The comedy of the time comes next, featuring selections from *Mad* magazine and *National Lampoon*.

What was youth culture like in late 1972? The next two magazines, *Teen* and *Teen World*, provide a glimpse into the questions and issues teens of the time were wrestling with.

Next come the news magazines - *Time*, *Newsweek*, and *Life* - in order to understand the political, financial, and cultural spirit of the time.

The print media concludes with sports (*Sports Illustrated*) and "entertainment for men" (*Playboy*). Since none of the centerfold pictures are included, you can truly say that you are reading *Playboy* for the articles.

The visual media for this section include a VH1 documentary on the music and culture of 1972, as well as the Apollo 17 prelaunch news coverage from December 5th and 6th.

While I have grouped the print and visual media in this way, you certainly don't have to, and can feel free to skip between the items you want to read or see first. In keeping with the methodology of Time Travel Simplified, you should complete the modules for this section (by writing them out in this book or just thinking about them) before moving onto the next section, which specifically examines *The Day* - December 7th 1972.

Enjoy!

THIRTY CENTS

NOVEMBER 22, 1963

Washington Hostesses

TIME

THE WEE   AGAZINE

NICOLE
ALPHAND

VOL. 82 NO. 21
(REG. U.S. PAT. OFF.)

JFK in Dallas - November 22, 1963

Module 1 - Kennedy's morning in Dallas - November 22, 1963
What are your thoughts as you watch this footage from the morning of November 22nd? What do you know already about the assassination of President Kennedy? Does this video change or enhance your knowledge of the event?

Time - November 22, 1963

Module 2 - The Presidency
President Kennedy "aged his Secret Service detail ten years" in the week prior to his assassination. What exactly did he do to accomplish that? And what was President Kennedy's primary political agenda in the week before his death?

Note: This particular *Time* magazine was delivered to Dr. Robert Guenther in Dallas, Texas on November 22, 1963! Dr. Guenther served as a Captain in the Army during World War II, and was awarded a Silver Star for his bravery at the Batle of the Bulge. After the war he practiced dentistry for 43 years, and passed away in 2004.

February 1964 35¢

COSMOPOLITAN

THEME OF THIS ISSUE: THE MARRIED AND THE UNMARRIED

THE ANATOMY

THE PLIGHT OF PRETTY GIRLS IN ENGLAND

Billion-Dollar War Between the Sexes

Begum Aga Khan Tells Her Love Story

LILLIAN WHITE DEER A CONDENSED NOVEL

Lolita meets up with Mark Antony in Mexico

SPECIAL REPORT **PROFILE OF OUR FIRST LADY**

Beatles in America - February 9, 1964

Module 3 - *The Ed Sullivan Show* - February 9, 1964
 If you were a teenager in 1964, The Beatles coming to America was big news! Watching their first appearance on *The Ed Sullivan Show*, what are your thoughts? Is the hype worth it? And are you convinced that Aero Shave and Griffin Liquid Wax are two of the luckiest companies in the history of advertising?

Cosmopolitan magazine - February 1964

Module 4 - Marriage and sex in America
 This is a pre-Helen Gurley Brown edition of *Cosmopolitan* (she would take over the magazine in 1965), but she still makes it into the article for her *Lessons in Love* book, which "discourses about such matters as how to have an affair, how to talk to a man in bed, how to get a girl to the brink [!], and how to keep her this way if you're not going to marry her."
 What are your thoughts about how "relationship" information should be presented to children and teens? Through their parents? Through the schools? Over the internet? And how do you believe this information has changed from the culture of 1964 to our time?

Moon Landing - July 20, 1969

Module 5 - Liftoff! - July 16, 1969

This was the "big one!" Although Apollo 10 had come within 47,000 feet of the moon's surface in a lunar lander piloted by future Apollo 17 astronaut Eugene Cerner, THIS was the mission that would land the first humans on the moon! What are your thoughts as you watch the launch? How did America make it to this point in less than a decade?

Sports Illustrated - July 14, 1969

Module 6 - O.J. is a holdout

O.J. Simpson became famous in football and infamous later, but in 1969 he was a holdout because the worst team in football (the Buffalo Bills, 1-12-1 for the 1968 season) wouldn't meet his demand for a five-year $650,000 contract. They were offering $250,00 for the same five years. My favorite quote in this article comes from O.J.'s manager Chuck Barnes, who said, "all of a sudden we might have O.J. as the bad guy, which is ridiculous." O.J. as the bad guy. Unthinkable.

For this module, research how the contract dispute worked out and what O.J.'s first few seasons were like. Reflect also on his Hollywood career, if you are familiar with it.

22

Ms. magazine - November 1972

Ms. magazine began publishing in 1972, but one of the first problems was coming up with what to call it. According to co-founder Gloria Steinem, the magazine was originally going to be called *Sojourner*, in honor of Sojourner Truth, a female abolitionist and women's rights advocate. That name was dismissed in the fear that the public would think it was a travel magazine. The next name candidate was *Sisters*, but it was dismissed because it was thought to sound like a Catholic religious magazine. Sheila Michaels, who popularized the use of "Ms." as a default form of address for women (whether they were married or not) pushed that as the name of the magazine, and it was chosen because it was short, symbolic, and was thought to lend itself easily to a logo.

A first trial edition of *Ms*. was published as an insert in *New York* magazine in December 1971, and it brought in 26,000 subscriptions. While Gloria Steinem originally conceived *Ms*. as a newsletter, she was convinced to publish it as a magazine. In her own words, "I realized as a journalist that there really was nothing for women to read that was controlled by women, and this caused me, along with a number of other women to start *Ms*. magazine."

The November 1972 cover features five women serving in the WACs, or Women's Army Corps. Formed in 1943 from its predecessor, the Women's Auxiliary Army Corps (or WAACs), the WACs, along with the Navy's WAVES, provided a way for women to serve in the armed forces. Although men were drafted into the military until July 1973, the WACs were an all-volunteer force of 13,000 women in 1972. Their reasons for joining the Army were, as the article says, "as a means of escape, of upward mobility, a place to learn a skill." But how were they as soldiers? No less of an authority than General Douglas McArthur said that they worked harder, complained less, and were more disciplined than the male draftees. The WACs were disbanded in 1978, and all of the units were integrated with existing, previously all-male units.

There are six modules associated with this *Ms*. - complete any or all of them.

Module 7: How to make trouble - environmentalism

The environmental movement has a long history, but one of the issues has been how ordinary people can get involved. This article explicates the measures people can take to bring change to the system. Do you think that the advice presented in the article remains relevant today? How have organizational methods and lobbying changed since 1972? And how have the results turned out?

Module 8: Confessions of a Househusband

Parenting is never easy in any era, but childcare was mostly the preserve of women in 1972. How does this article reinforce or refute gender stereotypes from our day? If you have children, how does the author's characterization of staying home with children compare to your experience?

Module 9: Child care according to Chairman Mao

The Cultural Revolution raged in China from 1966 until Mao's death in 1976. While exact figures are lacking, somewhere between hundreds of thousands to millions of people were killed in an attempt to purge "traditional" and "capitalist" elements from Chinese society. So what did they think about childcare? For this module, you should critically exam the arguments made by Ruth Sidel about childcare in Chinese society and the ramifications for raising children in America. Which aspects do you feel are valid and which should be abandoned?

Module 10: Mary Self-Worth

There may be no better cultural document of 1972 than the Mary Self-Worth cartoon. If it was in *National Lampoon*, it would clearly be satire, but it is so earnest and unfunny that it seems to be genuine. How are people portrayed in this comic strip? How are parents different from their children? What is youth culture like? How about the relationships between men and women? Or the advice given by the counselor?

Module 11: Being over 40

While it could be argued that every culture is a "youth culture," one of the beliefs of the 1960s was to not trust anyone over 30. So what is a woman in her 40s to do? Do you feel that things have changed for women older than 40 in our society? What aspects of Rollie Hochstein's article still ring true, and which are now historical artifacts?

Module 12: Advertising

Since advertisers choose which magazines they wish to appear in, I find the ads in individual magazines to be fascinating. In looking over this sample of ads from *Ms*., which do you think are still relevant and which are outdated? Is the target market still the same?

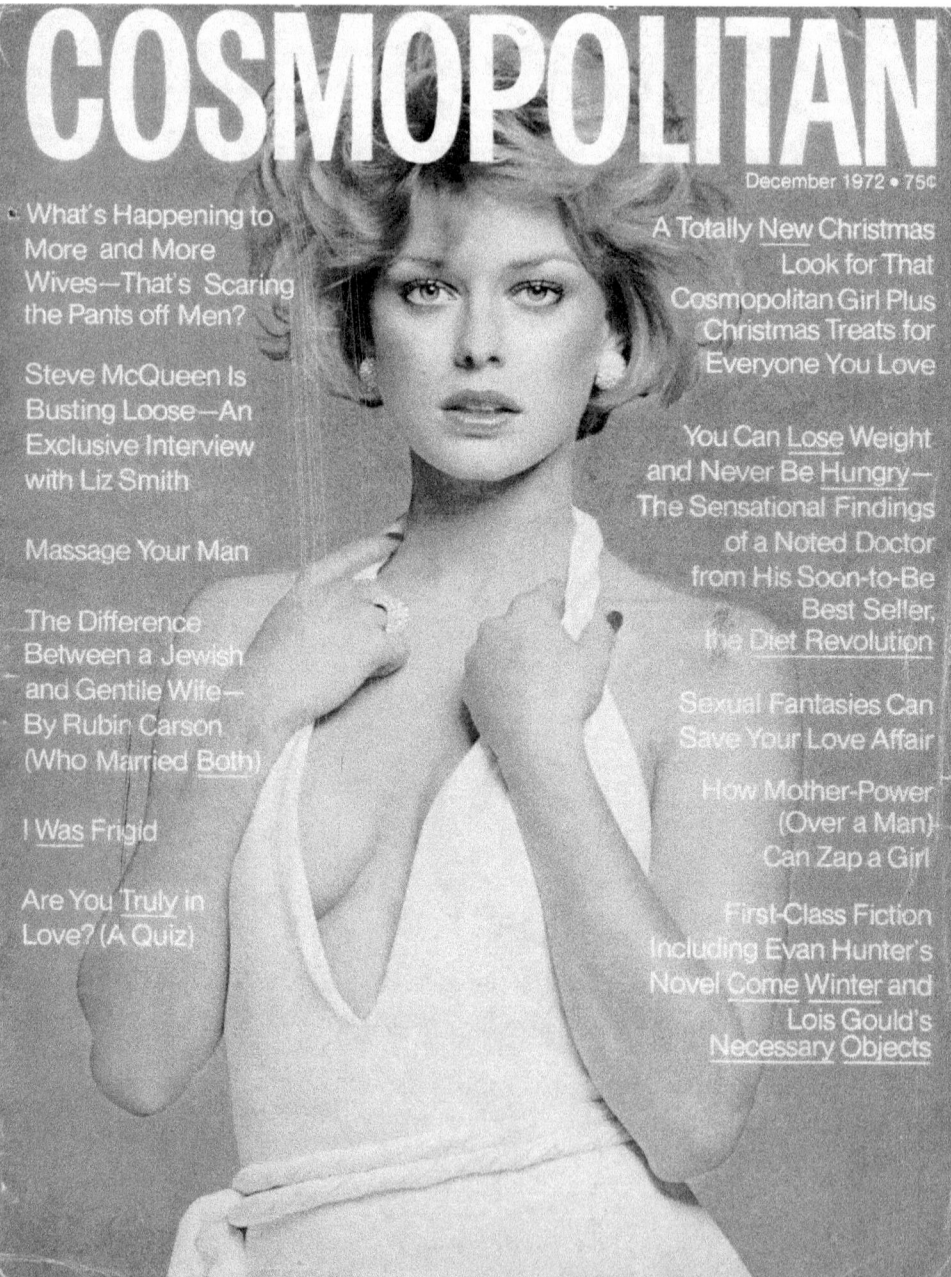

COSMOPOLITAN

December 1972 • 75¢

What's Happening to More and More Wives—That's Scaring the Pants off Men?

Steve McQueen Is Busting Loose—An Exclusive Interview with Liz Smith

Massage Your Man

The Difference Between a Jewish and Gentile Wife— By Rubin Carson (Who Married Both)

I Was Frigid

Are You Truly in Love? (A Quiz)

A Totally New Christmas Look for That Cosmopolitan Girl Plus Christmas Treats for Everyone You Love

You Can Lose Weight and Never Be Hungry— The Sensational Findings of a Noted Doctor from His Soon-to-Be Best Seller, The Diet Revolution

Sexual Fantasies Can Save Your Love Affair

How Mother-Power (Over a Man) Can Zap a Girl

First-Class Fiction Including Evan Hunter's Novel Come Winter and Lois Gould's Necessary Objects

Cosmopolitan - December 1972

While *Cosmopolitan* started as a "family" magazine in 1886, it didn't become a cultural phenomenon until Helen Gurley Brown became chief editor in 1965. She referred to herself as a "devout feminist," had written the bestseller *Sex and the Single Girl* in 1962, and managed to turn *Cosmopolitan* into THE magazine for successful single women. She was a firm believer in sexual liberation, and promoted the idea that single women should enjoy sex without any feelings of shame or guilt.

Helen Gurley Brown's spent thirty-two years with *Cosmopolitan*, and personally, I think the covers printed today look pretty interchangeable with those from 1972. And the story topics tend to remain the same - sexual tricks to make your partner scream in ecstasy, celebrity interviews, losing weight, relationship quizzes, and astrology. As I'm writing this in 2020, they're running an article on what a total Sagittarius Taylor Swift is! She even wrote a song called "The Archer" (the Sagittarius symbol)!

The December 1972 cover features model Randi Oakes, who at the time was in a long-term dating relationship with New York Jets quarterback Joe Namath. However, she's probably best known for her role as Officer Bonnie Clark from 1979 to 1982 on the NBC California highway patrol series *CHiPs*. She married actor Gregory Harrison, and retired from acting in 1985 when she began having children.

While this issue of *Cosmopolitan* doesn't feature any nude centerfolds of Burt Reynolds on a bearskin rug (that would be the April 1972 issue), it remains a good example of a woman's magazine of its time.

There are seven modules associated with this issue of *Cosmopolitan*. Complete any or all of them.

Module 13: I was frigid

This article does a good job of representing the reader Helen Gurley Brown was trying to appeal to with *Cosmopolitan*. Do you think that the experience of the writer is universal? Or is it tied to the era she was raised in? If you were her friend, what advice would you give her? As a romantic relationships researcher, I think the biggest "red flag" for me in the article is the quote, "Although I believed I loved Donald, the hostility and anger were still there . . . but I hid my feelings carefully until after we were married."

Module 14: The Analyst's Couch

Paging Dr. Freud! This column, by psychoanalyst Renatus Hartogs, provides a typical-for-its-time Freudian explanation of the husband's behavior. How would you interpret the husband's motivations and what advice would you provide? As a further note, according to an article in the June 19, 1972 *New York* magazine, Dr. Hartogs was sued by a former patient for "forcing her to have sexual relations with him 'under the guise' of psychiatric treatment."

Module 15: Gentile vs. Jewish Marriage

If you're interested in reading a check-list story full of sexist and anti-Semitic stereotypes, look no further! The article is written by Rubin Carson, and it's him comparing his first wife (who was Jewish) to his second wife (who was not) on six different criteria, including mood swings, cooking, and "sexual accessibility." Carson is Jewish, and references *Portnoy's Complaint*, a 1972 film starring actor Richard Benjamin. The movie, based on a 1969 book of the same name, is the sexual musings of a Jewish man about assimilating into American culture. While many hold the book in high regard, the movie was universally panned, with Roger Ebert calling it "a true fiasco," Gene Siskel giving it a "depressing" single star, and Vincent Canby of the *New York Times* describing it as "an unqualified disaster." While I beleive the same criticisms could be made about this *Cosmopolitan* article, I decided to include it because it is a "jaw-dropper" in terms of subject, language, and stereotypes. That it was published in an avowed feminist magazine is amazing to me. But what do you think? Are the comparisons funny? Is it anti-Semetic? Is the author revealing deeper truths or just repeating common stereotypes?

Module 16: Are You Truly in Love? - A quiz!

Cosmopolitan is famous for "relationship quizzes," and this edition of the magazine doesn't disappoint, with questions like "His lovemaking . . ." followed by multiple choice examples. Take the quiz yourself (adjusted for gender and circumstance) and see how you turn out with your significant other. Are you truly in love?

Module 17: Don Juan meets the 1970s

While they would be referred to as "players" in our era, men who attempt to juggle a number of women simultaneously have always existed. The article talks about how many of these men are television producers, film directors, photographers and agents. How has the "Me Too" era exposed these men? Has anything changed in the intervening years?

Module 18: Last Saturday Night

If you want to see who was a celebrity in December 1972, this feature will fill you in. It even has Peggy Lipton from *The Mod Squad*! What is your favorite answer and what were YOU doing at midnight last Saturday night?

Module 19: Advertising

In looking over this sample of ads from *Cosmopolitan*, which is your favorite? Why? Is it an ad that you think could still run today? Why or why not? And what do you think of the Burt Reynolds look-alike?

30

Mad magazine - December 1972

Soon after *Mad* magazine began publishing in 1952, a reader wrote in, "What you publish is cheap, miserable trash. Fortunately, I also am cheap, miserable trash!" Thus was the tone set for the multi-decade run of a magazine written by "the usual gang of idiots."

Mad began in a comic book format before switching to a magazine in 1955. The reason? Censorship. In the early 1950's Fredric Werthham wrote about the destructiveness of comic books on the minds of children in his book *Seduction of the Innocent*. Comics publishers switched to self-censorship of their material, but by changing the dimensions of the product (from comic book to magazine), *Mad* was able to become a satire magazine and dodge the censorship. Since *Mad* carried no interior advertising from 1957 until 2001, there were no advertisers to offend, and so the writers were unhindered and able to produce the work they wanted and loved.

The switch from comic book to magazine also brought mascot Alfred E. Neuman to the cover of almost every issue. Originally modeled after a face used in early 20th century ads for "painless dentistry," the Neuman mascot was conceived as a "visual logo" in the same way as the Jolly Green Giant. His motto of "What, me worry?" was derived from the same "painless dentistry" ads, which I think makes it even funnier.

Mad was not published monthly, but rather eight times a year, with double issues for Jan/Feb, March/April, July/Aug, and Oct/Nov. Another interesting anomaly was that issues would come out up to two months before the date on the magazine, so that the December issue would come out in October. It's mad! *Mad* stopped publishing new material in 2019, but it was an incredibly popular magazine in the early 1970s, with a peak circulation of 2.8 million in 1973.

The December 1972 cover features the wedding scene from *The Godfather*, with Alfred E. Neuman as the "gun boy." Although it came out in March, *The Godfather* was the most popular movie of 1972. Also featured in this issue is a spoof of the *Mary Tyler Moore Show*, which at the time was in its third season and a Top 10 show in the Nielson ratings.

There are four modules associated with this issue of *Mad*. Complete any or all of them.

Module 20: The Oddfather

If you haven't seen *The Godfather* (and *The Godfather: Part 2*), then you have a wonderful viewing experience ahead of you! Even if you haven't seen it in awhile, the idea of an "Italian Mafia Family" has worked its way into mainstream American culture. What stereotypes of Italian-Americans are suggested in this satire? Could they be made today? And how well does this piece follow the storyline of the movie? Personally, I find the caricatures of the actors to be spot-on. How are their performance styles mocked throughout?

Module 21: *The Mary Tailor-Made Show*

I would have to rewatch the show to get a sense of how much of a "clothes horse" MTM is on her show, but in the *Mad* satire, it seems to be one of the main reasons for the entire series. Reading it now, do you believe that this satire is sexist against the female characters? Why or why not? What about the names chosen for the characters? What would be a more tasteful name for "Rodent?" And what about the criticisms of the way news is portrayed? Has anything changed since 1972?

Module 22: Protest Signs

Mad became more overtly political in the early 1970s, as this and the next module show. How many of the people are you able to recognize from their caricatures? And which is your favorite sign combination? Why? Which combinations do you think would be considered offensive to an audience today?

Module 23: Campaign Instant Phrasemakers

This is my favorite feature in the December 1972 edition of *Mad* magazine because it is, in my opinion, the most timeless. The same exact phrases (now referred to as "talking points") have been in circulation forever. What was your favorite phrase you generated? Could it be used in today's political climate? Why or why not?

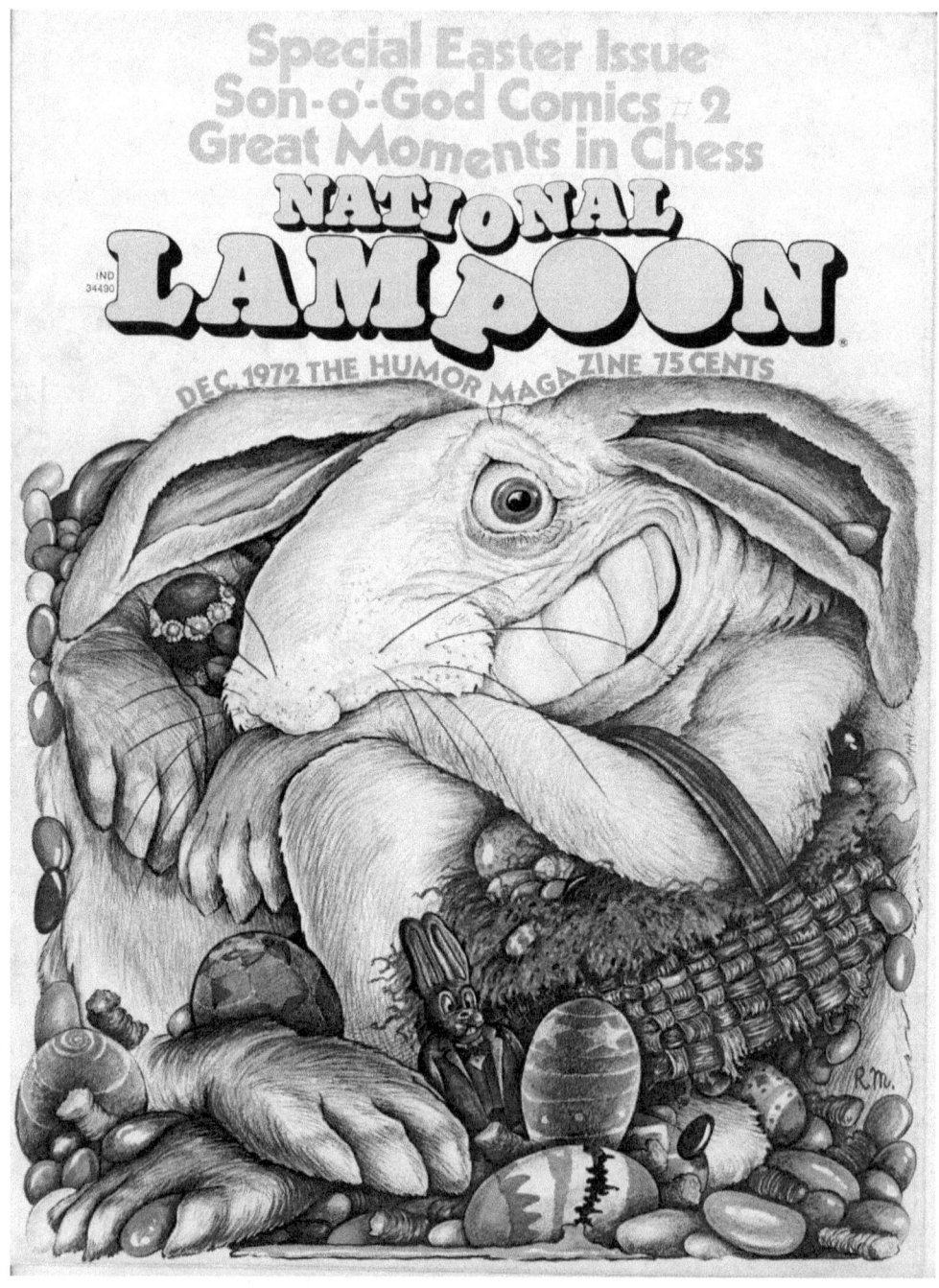

National Lampoon - December 1972

National Lampoon grew out of *The Harvard Lampoon*, which has been described as "a famous thing that no one has ever seen a copy of." Started in 1876, it boasted of having had writers John Updike and George Plimpton as editors. However, it wasn't in any sense a national publication.

That changed in the late 1960s when Doug Kenney and Henry Beard took over. Described by contemporaries as "incredibly brilliant, incredibly funny, and incredibly good friends," their big break came when they got a call from Betsy Talbot Blackwell, the editor of *Mademoiselle*. She offered them $7,000 and a subscription insert in *Mademoiselle* if they would produce a parody version of the magazine as a single-issue insert. They did, and it was a huge hit. *Harvard Lampoon* parody issues of *Time*, *Playboy*, Life, and *Sports Illustrated* soon followed.

The success of the parody issues made Kenney and Beard realize that there was a market for their style of humor. They got a financial backer who took 75% of the profit and the right to buy them out in 5 years, and *National Lampoon* was born. The first issue came out in April 1970, and the magazine became immensely popular, with national circulation peaking at a million copies per month in 1974.

The December 1972 issue is of course devoted to Easter, which is why the Easter Bunny is on the cover and "Son-o'-God" comics are inside.

There are five modules associated with this edition of *National Lampoon*. Complete any or all of them.

Module 24: True Facts
The True Facts section of *National Lampoon* was a popular and long-running selection of "bizarre but true" news stories sent in by readers, who received a free year of the magazine if their news clipping was used. A number of True Facts compilation books were published over the years (and I own some of them). Which is your favorite story from this issue? Why?

Module 25: Four more years of Nixon jokes
Richard Nixon had won re-election the previous month. While all of the news in this section is made up, much of it is prescient. Which is your favorite item? Which do you think could best describe the world that we live in now?

Module 26: Dr. Trow's Schools
We live in a time of for-profit colleges and distance learning for what are often junk degrees. So here's more! Which classes would you like to take or franchise? Which is the funniest idea? The Fat School? Therapeutic Drug Community? Can't-Dance-School? How about the Alternate Academy - "Yes, RICH KIDS are eager to TURN ON TO POVERTY!"

Module 27: Inventions that never made it

  While many of these are just silly, they're all pretty funny, and I'm not sure why someone hasn't marketed "tomato chips" yet. It's not a bad idea! Which of the "inventions" is your favorite? Why? How would you market such an invention?

Module 28: Son-o'-God comics

  The 1970s were clearly a different time, and a comic like this could never be published today. What do you think is the most offensive aspect of this comic?

38

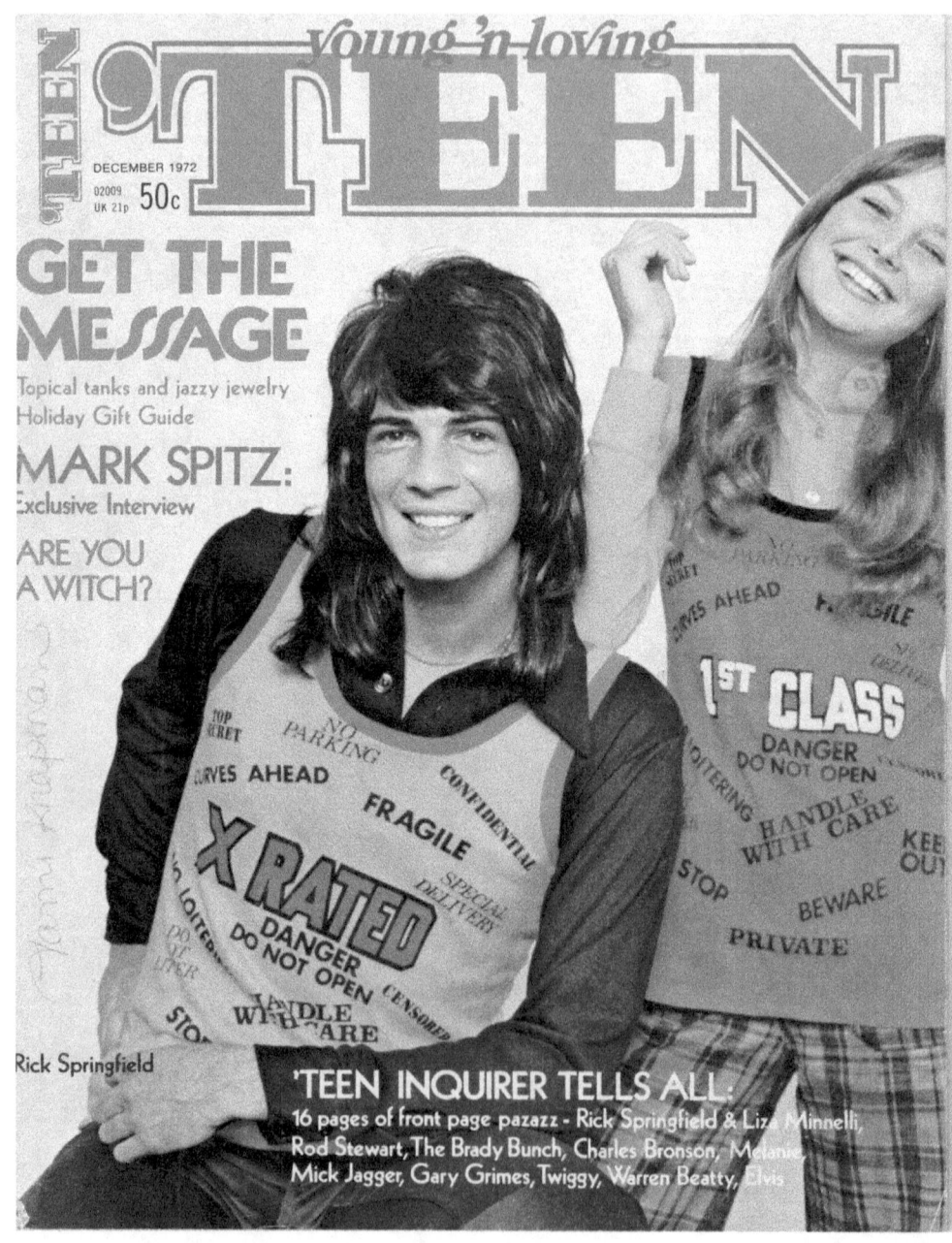

young 'n loving

TEEN

DECEMBER 1972
02009
UK 21p 50c

GET THE MESSAGE

Topical tanks and jazzy jewelry
Holiday Gift Guide

MARK SPITZ:
Exclusive Interview

ARE YOU
A WITCH?

Rick Springfield

'TEEN INQUIRER TELLS ALL:
16 pages of front page pazazz - Rick Springfield & Liza Minnelli,
Rod Stewart, The Brady Bunch, Charles Bronson, Melanie,
Mick Jagger, Gary Grimes, Twiggy, Warren Beatty, Elvis

Teen magazine - December 1972

Not to be confused with *Teen World* magazine, "young 'n loving" *Teen* began publishing in 1954 and was aimed at girls in their early teen years. While it featured a host of entertainment news, advice columns, and fashion tips, it also strove to cover teen culture and happenings.

Are the stories which appear in the December 1972 issue of *Teen* true? Are there 100,000 Americans, "many of them teens," practicing "witchcraft or Satanism?" Is Charles Bronson, at 51 years old, the "World's Sexiest, Richest, HOTTEST Actor?" These questions and many other are covered in the modules below.

The cover features Rick Springfield, a person who I thought I knew some things about, but with a little research found out that I knew nothing about. First, I thought he was American, but actually he's from Australia. Second, I thought that he wasn't a singer until the early 1980's with his hit "Jessie's Girl," which won him the Grammy Award for Best Male Rock Vocal Performance. Since he's on the cover of *Teen* in 1972, he was obviously a star prior to 1981. Springfield (although his actual name is Springthorpe) got his start in the Australian band Zoot, which broke up in May 1971. He moved to the United States and released the hit single "Speak to the Sky," which peaked at number 14 on the Billboard Hot 100 chart in September 1972. So that's how he got on the cover of *Teen*. Plus, he was only 23 at the time, and so more-or-less age-appropriate (especially compared to "sexy" Charles Bronson) for the readership of the magazine. The 1970s weren't the best for Rick Springfield - although he was promoted as a pop star in the mold of Donny Osmond or David Cassidy, his albums bombed, and he was reduced to performing in the ABC Saturday morning cartoon series *Mission: Magic!* He had a great 1980s though, with hit albums and a starring role as Dr. Noah Drake on the daytime soap opera *General Hospital*. Since I consider him much more of an 80s star, the "hunk" module is about Mark Spitz, who personifies the 1972 Summer Olympics.

There are four modules associated with this edition of *Teen*. Complete any or all of them.

Module 29: Jack and Jill advice columns

Who do you turn to when you're 16, married, and pregnant? An advice columnist! The Jack and Jill advice columns don't get easy-to-answer questions, but they they do their best in the answers. What do you think are the best questions and answers from each column? Which questions would you have answered differently? Why?

Module 30: Mark Spitz

I was only six years old in 1972, but even I remember Mark Spitz! After breaking 28 world records and winning seven Olympic gold medals at the Summer Olympics, he was part of the national conversation for months. While this article is more about trying to get an interview, it does ask the hard-hitting questions like "What does Mark think of girls in general?" How does Spitz come across in the article? Research how his life changed after swimming.

Module 31: Charles Bronson

What starts out as a fluff piece on a 51-year-old "sex symbol" in a magazine aimed at teenagers ends very differently. How does Bronson regard his own stardom? While he was a box office star by 1972, research the roles that he turned down - they're pretty amazing.

Module 32: Are you a witch?

Who knew that in 1972 witchcraft and Satanism were sweeping up teens throughout America?! What are your thoughts about this article? Is the research valid? What about the people interviewed? After reading the article, what do you think people in 1972 would have thought? What do you think now?

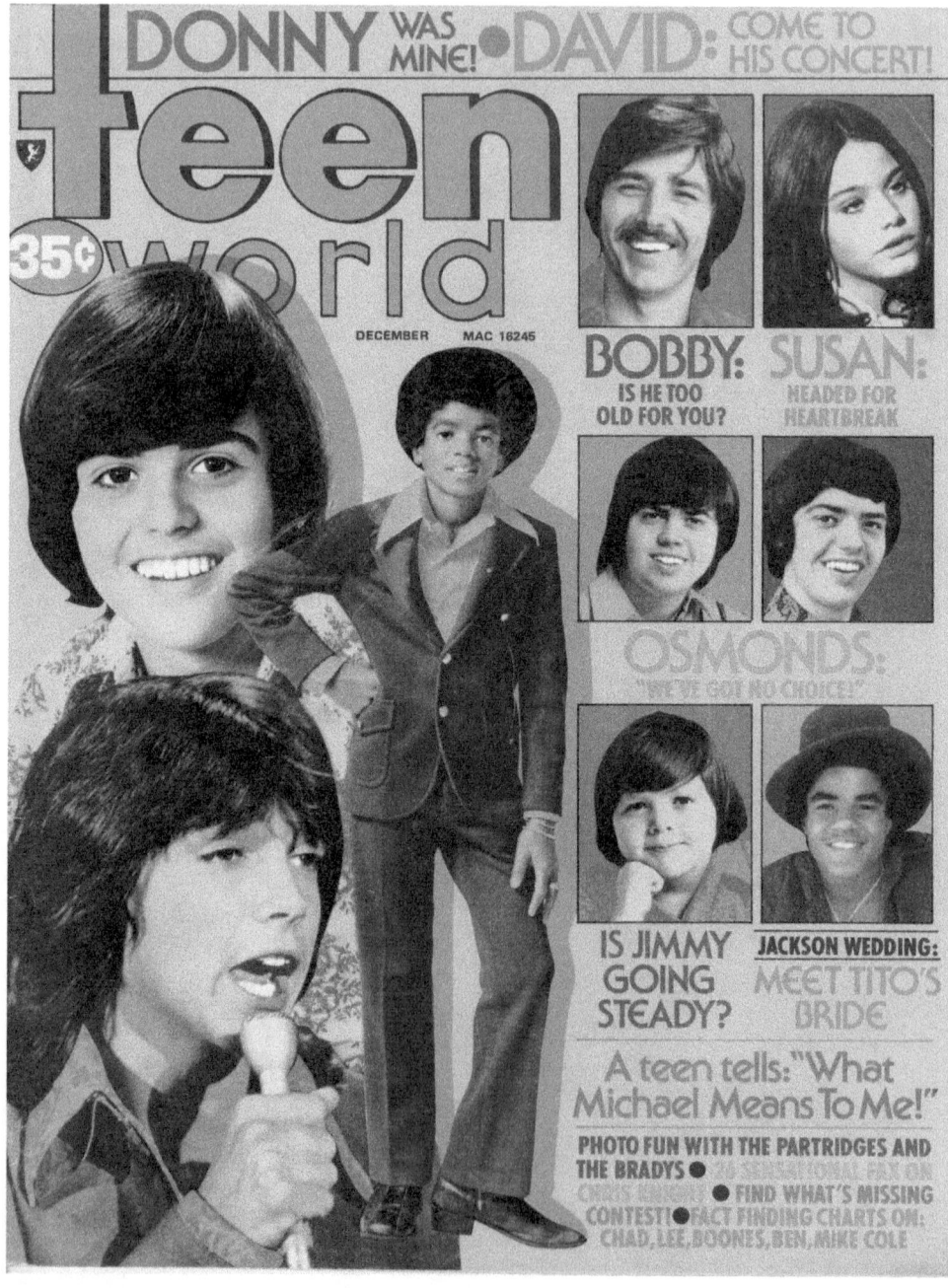

DONNY WAS MINE! • DAVID: COME TO HIS CONCERT!

teen world

35¢

DECEMBER   MAC 16245

BOBBY: IS HE TOO OLD FOR YOU?

SUSAN: HEADED FOR HEARTBREAK

OSMONDS: "WE'VE GOT NO CHOICE!"

IS JIMMY GOING STEADY?

JACKSON WEDDING: MEET TITO'S BRIDE

A teen tells: "What Michael Means To Me!"

PHOTO FUN WITH THE PARTRIDGES AND THE BRADYS ● 20 SENSATIONAL FAX ON CHRIS KNIGHT ● FIND WHAT'S MISSING CONTEST! ● FACT FINDING CHARTS ON: CHAD, LEE, BOONES, BEN, MIKE COLE

Teen World magazine - December 1972

Reading *Teen World* will make you cringe. Whether it is an article about the Osmonds where they're all dressed up like Elvis in white leather rhinestone jackets or an article asking whether singer Bobby Sherman "is too old for you?" (since he was 29 at the time, I'd say he was too old for a teen, but that's my opinion), *Teen World* is guaranteed to make an adult shudder.

Rather than discussing this magazine in depth, let's go straight to the modules. There are four modules associated with this edition of *Teen World*. Complete any or all of them.

Module 33: What Michael Means to Me
        This article is actually (according to the editor's note) a letter from Bonnie H. in Georgia to *Teen World* about her love of Michael Jackson. Do you think that this letter is legitimate or was it written by the editors? How common of a phrase was "dig" in 1972? Regardless, compare and contrast the feelings of a teen from 1972 with your beliefs about Michael Jackson. What are the similarities and differences?

Module 34: TW Salutes Four Fabulous Faves
        They all happen to be men in their 30s, but Michael Cole (32), Chad Everett (35), Ben Murphy (30), and Lee Majors (33) are the focus of this article written for teens. Of the four, who do you think is likely to have the largest teen audience? Who do you think was able to have the most sustainable career?

Module 35: Pen Pals
        In a magazine full of questionable content, this spread takes the prize - teens with pictures, a blurb about them, and their address. It's not difficult to imagine how this plays out in a "To Catch a Predator" sense. Putting that aside, who would you most like to write to? Why?

Module 36: Advertisements
        From these ads, teens seem to have a lot of extra cash and not many qualms about how to spend it. Which is your favorite advertisement? Which do you believe is the biggest scam? Why?

44

Time magazine - December 4, 1972

Started by Briton Hadden and Henry Luce, two editors from the *Yale Daily News* in 1923, *Time* was originally going to be called *Facts*. Their goal was to create a weekly newsmagazine that could be read in an hour. The idea was to report the news through a focus on people, which is why for decades the cover of *Time* featured a single person.

Our December 4th issue is no different, with "Hollywood's New Nordic Star" Liv Ullman on the cover. Although she was born in Tokyo (her father was an aircraft engineer working there in 1938) and spent much of her childhood in the United States, she became famous for starring in the films of Swedish director Ingmar Bergman. She won the Golden Globe for Best Actress three months after her appearance on the cover of *Time* for her part in the film *The Emigrants*.

I find this edition interesting for the in-depth articles included in the modules below.

There are five modules associated with this edition of *Time*. Complete any or all of them.

Module 37: Paris Peace talks and the Viet Cong view
This issue of *Time* provides both an analysis of the Paris Peace Talks and an interview with Nguyen Thi Binh, the head of the Viet Cong delegation. How accurate do you feel the information provided by *Time* and Mme. Bihn is? Research her future career in Vietnam. Also, what about Kissinger's "Briarcliff-grad blonde" friend Jan Cushing? Her future (as Jan Amory) is fascinating and worth looking into ("Afternoon of a Golden Girl" from 2003).

Module 38: Who pays for the U.N.?
United Nations funding is a perennial "hot-button" issue in U.S. politics. Research the level of American contributions to the U.N. in our time compared to 1972. Do you believe that this remains a controversial issue? If so, how would you propose to resolve it? If not, why shouldn't it be controversial?

Module 39: A hard ruling for software
Readers in 1972 had to be told that a computer "program" was "a set of mathematical instructions." We all know who eventually won the "hardware" vs. "software" argument, but why do you think software became so important? Research where Bill Gates and Steve Jobs were in 1972 - you'll be amazed.

Module 40: The Bennington Couple
As someone who works in higher education myself, I can say that the idea of someone becoming a college president at age 29 is pretty amazing. How do you feel about the way Gail and Tom Parker are presented in this article? What changes did they seek to make to Bennington? Research how things turned out for them.

Module 41: Blue-collar pundit

Every era seems to have a "blue-collar pundit." Who is ours? And what do you think of Mike Lavelle's views on class conflict and "Women's Lib?" How are his views on politics similar to "blue collar" people of our own time?

December 4, 1972   50 cents

Newsweek

THE RUNNING BACKS

The Redskins'
Larry Brown

Newsweek - December 4, 1972

One of the things you'll notice about *Newsweek* is that except for the financial columns, none of the articles have a reporter byline. This is a characteristic of the era in magazines (you'll notice that the newspapers identify the reporter who wrote a particular article). What was unique about *Newsweek* was that of the 51 reporters who wrote for the magazine, only one was a woman. She was Liz Peer, and she was initially hired as a "copy girl" in 1958. When she asked about becoming a reporter, she was told that if she wanted to write she needed to go elsewhere. Her break came in 1961, when the *Washington Post* bought *Newsweek*, and she was given a "tryout" as a reporter - the only woman who was given the opportunity. In 1964 she was appointed as a foreign correspondent based in Paris, and at the time of this issue, was a reporter in *Newsweek's* Washington D.C. bureau.

A lawsuit was filed in 1970 by Eleanor Holmes Norton (an ACLU attorney) with the Equal Opportunity Employment Commission on behalf of sixty women who worked at *Newsweek* as researchers, alleging that the disparity in reporter positions was a "blatant policy of discrimination against women." *Newsweek* signed an agreement to settle the case on August 26th, 1970, promising to give women equal opportunity to become reporters within one year. A *Newsweek* spokesman said that it was "absolutely coincidental" that the agreement was signed on the same day as a "Strike for Equity" organized by Women's Liberation groups. In a further irony, *Newsweek's* cover story for that week was about the feminist movement, entitled "Women in Revolt." The article was written by freelance reporter Helen Dudar because the *Newsweek* editors didn't believe that Liz Peer (the only female reporter at the magazine) was qualified to write the article. In a final irony, Eleanor Holmes Norton, who initially filed the suit, was appointed as the first female Chair of the Equal Opportunity Employment Commission in 1977. She currently (as of 2020) serves in the U. S. House of Representatives as a non-voting delegate representing the District of Columbia.

This week's cover was painted by artist LeRoy Neiman. He got his start in the 1950's doing freelance illustrations for a department store where Hugh Heffner was also working as an ad writer. That started a fifty year collaboration with *Playboy* magazine, where Neiman created the "femlin" character (who appeared on the *Party Jokes* page) and did a 15-year series of paintings of his visits to exotic locations called "Man at His Leisure."

Neiman eventually turned to sports events and athletes, and would paint on-air for ABC's *Monday Night Football*. While commercially successful, he was ridiculed for working too fast, using vulgar color schemes, and creating lowbrow art for people who don't know anything about art. He took it in good humor though. When one critic said that he created paintings fit for hotel rooms, his response was "What's wrong with paintings in hotel rooms?"

My favorite criticism of his painting comes from the 1984 movie *Top Secret*, where the "bad-guy" Germans are torturing the hero trying to get information. A General asks if they've gotten any information from him yet and a soldier responds, "They're still working on him. He won't break. We've tried everything! Do you want me to bring out the LeRoy Neiman paintings?" The general responds, "No. We cannot risk violating the Geneva Convention."

There are five modules associated with this *Newsweek*. Complete any or all of them.

Module 42: The Periscope
The Periscope was a *Newsweek* section devoted to news rumors and innuendo. For this module, read through the nine news bits and then pick one to research and see how things turned out.

Module 43: Stocks and the Dow Jones Industrial Average
The Dow first hit 1000 on November 14, 1972, three weeks prior to this issue of *Newsweek*. One of the interesting things to me is the issues that they are discussing (inclusion of stocks in the Dow, other indices like the S&P 500, and the ability to predict where the market is heading) are the same issues that we still discuss today. For this module, read through the columnists' analyses, make a prediction based upon your impressions, and then see where the Dow Jones Industrial Average was two years later (in December 1974) and ten years later (in December 1982).

Module 44: Vietnam Peace Talks in Paris
We know how the Vietnam War turned out, but for people at the time, trying to negotiate a peace proposal, things looked differently. For this module, read through *Newsweek's* analysis of the Paris Peace Talks and research how things turned out.

Module 45: Apollo 17 retrospective
This article provides a retrospective on the Apollo Program and highlights both the accomplishments and the future of U.S. space exploration. How did those predictions turn out? What has been the legacy of the Apollo Program? How were our lives made different by space exploration?

Module 46: Loretta Lynn
If you've seen the Academy Award winning 1980 film *Coal Miner's Daughter*, then you already know the story of Loretta Lynn's rise to country music fame. How does this article confirm or disagree with the portrait presented in the movie? Also, since we know her future, how were the rest of the 1970s for Loretta and Mooney? And if you have one, what is your favorite Loretta Lynn song?

LIFE

**With Henry Kissinger
in His Paris
'Battle Station'**

Mellow,
busy days
after the
White House

HARRY TRUMAN
by Margaret Truman

DECEMBER 1 · 1972 · 50¢

Life magazine - December 1, 1972

Former president Harry Truman was ailing in December 1972, and would pass before the end of the month (December 26th, to be exact). The December 1st *Life* magazine features a cover story by his daughter Margaret as a family-based retrospective on his life, but it's a bit of a "puff piece," and is not included in the modules.

There are three modules for this edition of *Life*. Complete any or all of them.

Module 47: Pieta restoration

Completed by Michelangelo in 1500, the Pieta was attacked on May 21, 1972 by 33-year-old geologist Laszlo Toth, who struck it with a sculptor's hammer 15 times while yelling "I am Jesus Christ! Risen from the dead!" *Life* magazine was actually incorrect in the specifics of Toth's apprehension. It was other tourists who wrestled him to the ground - the Vatican guards were pretty much useless on this occasion. Toth was placed in an Italian psychiatric hospital for two years, and no charges were ever filed against him. The article also fails to mention that many of the marble chips knocked off of the statue were pocketed by tourists who took them home, apparently as souvenirs. The nose of Mary had to be restored with marble from the back of the statue.

The restored Pieta was presented to the general public in March 1973 behind a triple layer of bullet-proof glass - proof that the barn door only gets shut after the horse has escaped. The closest tourists were allowed to come to the statue was 25 feet.

What do you think about the protection and preservation of priceless art objects? Should they be on display for the general public? Where is the balance between preservation and access?

Module 48: Kissinger in Paris

This is basically a photo spread of Kissinger negotiating the Paris Peace Accords. How is the tone and content of this article different from the presentations in *Time* and *Newsweek*?

Module 49: The Alsager children

By what criteria should children be removed from their parents' home? What level of abuse and neglect is necessary for the State to intervene? These were some of the issues involved in the case of Charles and Darline Alsager. Research how the case turned out on appeal. How do you think the case would be treated today?

ENTERTAINMENT FOR MEN

DECEMBER 1972 • $1.50

PLAYBOY

ENJOY OUR

Gala

CHRISTMAS ISSUE

NUTTY NEW HUMOR BY WOODY ALLEN • NEW WORKS BY BERNARD MALAMUD, LAWRENCE DURRELL, RAY BRADBURY, KINGSLEY AMIS, ROBERT GRAVES, NELSON ALGREN • MOVIE SEX STARS OF 1972 • AN INTERVIEW WITH YEVGENY YEVTUSHENKO • DAN GREENBURG GOES TO HIS FIRST ORGY • RALPH NADER, ROBERT TOWNSEND, MURRAY KEMPTON, ROBERT EVANS ON "POWER!" PLUS EVERYTHING FROM ALPHA WAVES TO PINBALL MACHINES TO MAFIA DONS

Playboy magazine - December 1972

If you grew up watching Hugh Heffner on the reality television series *The Girls Next Door* (which ran for 90 episodes from 2005-2009), then you probably don't realize the level of social philosopher he was considered to be in the 1960s and 70s. He even appeared on *Firing Line* in 1966, debating William F. Buckley over what was called "the Playboy philosophy."

The magazine got its start when Heffener was working as a copywriter at *Esquire* and was turned down for a $5 raise. He decided to mortgage his house and raise money from family and friends for a magazine that was originally going to be called *Stag Party*. The first issue of *Playboy* was released in December 1953 and featured a nude centerfold of Marilyn Monroe, taken in 1949, before she was famous. It sold 50,000 copies, and launched Heffner's publishing career. On a somewhat unrelated note, Heffner, who died in 2017 at the age of 91, is buried in the crypt next to Marilyn Monroe in the Westwood Memorial Park in Los Angeles. Although they never met in real life, he bought the crypt for $75k in 1992, telling the *Los Angeles Times* that "spending eternity next to Marilyn is an opportunity too sweet to pass up."

The cover is a parody of a Coca-Cola Christmas advertisement (with "Gala" in the same font) and runs to a whopping 346 pages, with most pages devoted to advertising. The December 1972 issue of *Playboy* represents Heffner's creation at its peak socially, culturally, and in terms of circulation. In 1972, even a braille edition of *Playboy* was available! I made a choice NOT to include any of the centerfold pictures from the December 1972 issue so that, like men of the time, we can say that we're reading *Playboy* for the articles.

There are seven modules associated with this edition of *Playboy*. Complete any or all of them.

Module 50: The Playboy Advisor

This is an "Ask us anything!" monthly feature of *Playboy*, and questions range from circumcised penises on statues in the Louvre to whether it is safe to smoke marijuana while pregnant. Which question and answer are your favorite? What do you think about the quality of the advice? Would you provide different answers?

Module 51: Forum Newsfront

The Forum Newsfront is a digest of news from all over the country which is "related to issues raised by 'the Playboy philosophy.'" Which piece of news do you find to the most interesting? And which is most relevant to our times?

Module 52: Head of the Family

This is an outstanding article about "Mr. Gribbs," Carmine Tramunti, the head of the Lucchese crime family, and the state of organized crime in America in the early 1970s. Again, it's a joke to say that you read *Playboy* for the articles, but this is a truly outstanding article. Research what happened as this article went to press, and the eventual fate of Mr. Gribbs.

Module 53: Party Jokes

Another monthly feature of Playboy are the jokes which follow the centerfold. The "femlin" cartoon women are drawn by LeRoy Neiman, who also illustrated the December 4th cover of *Newsweek*. Which joke is your favorite?

Module 54: Woody Allen

Playboy attracted articles from the top talent of the time, and this cartoon spread is further proof of it. Regardless of your views on Woody Allen, he was everywhere in 1972. The "Match Wits with Inspector Ford" piece is absurdist parody at its best - he later used some of the gags in his film *Love and Death*. Which "case" is your favorite and why?

Module 55: Healthcare in America

Although this is an advertisement for Aetna from 1972, it could have been written yesterday. Compare and contrast how the healthcare proposals from 1972 are the same and different from the proposals of our time.

Module 56: Advertising

Knowing that an advertisement would appear in *Playboy* seems to have had a huge impact on the companies running the ad campaigns. Which ads do you think are most effective? Why? Would any still work in our time?

58

Sports Illustrated - December 4, 1972

For anyone who loves sports, *Sports Illustrated* (or *SI*) has been a weekly source of sports news since 1954. The addition of the "swimsuit issue" in 1964 made *SI* part of the cultural conversation. However, the history of the magazine is more complicated.

The magazine was originally started in 1936 with a focus on "sportsmen," meaning a focus on golf, tennis, and boat racing (or all things!). The logistics of printing at the time meant that *SI* was a monthly, as the public had newspapers for daily sports news. When the original publisher sold *SI* in 1949, it only lasted another six issues.

It was Henry Luce, the publisher of *Time*, who saw the potential of the magazine. While many people advised him that there wasn't enough sports news to justify a weekly magazine, he felt that the time was right, and relaunched *Sports Illustrated* in 1954. Luce wasn't even a sports fan, and his critics were correct - *SI* lost money for over a decade. But the advent of televised sports created a market for the magazine. Right place, right time.

The cover of the December 4th issue features San Francisco quarterback (and punter) Steve Spurrier. While he spent a decade in the NFL, his real fame came as a head coach of college teams. Know by his nickname, "Head Ball Coach," Spurrier successfully ran the football programs at Duke, South Carolina, and Florida before his retirement in 2015. He even spent two years coaching the Washington Redskins!

There are four modules for this edition of *Sports Illustrated*. Complete any or all of them.

Module 57: Woody Hayes and Ohio State football
While there are a number of college football rivalries, few have been as intense as the Ohio State/Michigan contests of the early 1970s. Part of this was due to the personalities of the head coaches - Bo Schembechler and Woody Hayes. How does this article present the coaches and the game? Research Woody Hayes and his controversial actions and comments both on and off the football field. And research how the 1973 Rose Bowl turned out for Ohio State!

Module 58: Ali in Vegas
Muhammad Ali was a monumental cultural and sports figure, and won six (6!) fights in 1972. This article has it all - Ali, Vegas, Bill Cosby, and Issac Hayes. But they can't stop talking about Joe Frazier. Compare and contrast the portrayal of Ali, Las Vegas, and Bob Foster, and what boxing was like in 1972.

Module 59: Spring training
Hope always returns with Spring training and a new crop of rookie players. To truly enjoy this article, you might have to be a fan of rookie Keith Hernandez and the St. Louis Cardinals. Of all the players mentioned in this article, who made it big in "The Show?"

Module 60: Advertising

　　　　Cars, slacks, games, and drugs. *Sports Illustrated's* advertisers knew their target market. In this sample of ads, which is your favorite? Today, I can't even imagine how much I would be willing to pay to have an AMC Gremlin with Levi's denim seats!

VH1: *1972 - Behind the Music*

While a VH1 documentary about music and culture may not be the most academic source for history information, it has the virtue of being entertaining and providing context for the year 1972. I think it serves two other purposes too. First, it asserts that the social and political climate of a time impacts the culture and music of that same time. It asks the question of how music was impacted by the ongoing war in Vietnam, the reelection of President Nixon, and the Women's Liberation movement. Second, since the documentary was made in the late 1990's as a part of the *Behind the Music* series, it sought to translate an earlier time to a contemporary audience. Since we're now several decades beyond when the documentary was made, we can get insight into how 1972 was framed by people of the following generation - what was cool, what wasn't, and why.

There are three modules associated with this documentary.

Module 61: What did you learn?

What was the most surprising bit of information that you learned from this documentary? Was it new information, or just something you hadn't thought of in a while?

Module 62: Favorite music

While a LOT of music from 1972 is covered in this documentary, there are entire genres which are not discussed at all, such as country. While this is understandable given that VH1 focuses on pop music, it remains a deficit. After watching the documentary, which songs do you believe are the best from 1972? Why? Research the country hits from 1972 and see if you have some favorites there too!

Module 63: Time and timelessness

The documentary offers a number of portraits of artists popular in 1972. Who do you think has "aged" the best and is most relevant to our time? Why?

Prelaunch news coverage - December 5, 1972

While the footage isn't the greatest, the stories are powerful in these news reports from the day before the launch of Apollo 17. It's important to keep in mind that the launch was originally going to take place on the evening of December 6th, and was delayed until the early hours of December 7th.

The CBS footage features Walter Cronkite and interviews with each of the astronauts - Mission Commander Eugene Cernan, Lunar Module Pilot Jack Schmitt, and Command Module Pilot Ron Evans. Cronkite was a huge booster of the Space Program and as the "Most Trusted Man in America," more than half of the television sets tuned in to the 1969 moon landing were watching him on CBS.

Also included is footage of John Chancellor of NBC news, and Harry Reasoner of ABC news. There are four modules associated with this media.

Module 64: The Astronauts

Morton Dean of CBS interviews each of the astronauts before the flight. Which of them strikes you as the most interesting and engaging? Research the futures of each of them. What interesting facts did you find?

Module 65: The Desert Mice

Walter Cronkite does a story about the five (5) mice (*Perognathus longimembris*) who were a part of the Apollo 17 BIOCORE (BIOlogical COsmic Ray Experiment) research. Search to find the names of the mice and the results of the experiment!

Module 66: The crowds

John Dancy of NBC news has a report on the people who have been camping out to watch the nighttime launch of Apollo 17. How would you describe their demographics and their motivation for watching the launch?

Module 67: The changes to Coco Beach

Jules Bergman of ABC news has an interesting interview with a couple who have switched their business away from serving the space industry. They seem to have the ultimate 1970s business plan! What do you think of their prospects and how are they indicative of entrepreneurialism in our own time?

Prelaunch news coverage - December 6, 1972

Again, the footage isn't great, but the stories are. News coverage of the "day" of the launch provides more insight into the training of the astronauts and the history of the space program in the United States.

There are three modules associated with this media.

Module 68: "Not a hitch in sight"
Although Walter Cronkite begins his newscast by saying that there's "not a hitch in sight," the Apollo 17 launch was delayed by a "hitch" 30 seconds before launch - a first in the Apollo program. Research what the "hitch" was and how long it took to resolve!

Module 69: Astronaut training
Jules Bergman of ABC news has a report on the training of the astronauts and specifically on Dr. Jack Schmitt. What do you believe is the role for scientists in the study of space? Why is it important to have a trained geologist on the lunar surface? What other specializations would be helpful?

Module 70: Wernher von Braun interview
Apollo program director Sam Phillips was quoted as saying that the United States wouldn't have made it to the Moon as quickly without the work of Wernher von Braun. After discussing the quote with NASA colleagues, he changed it to say that without von Braun, we wouldn't have made it to the moon at all. Research this incredibly influential and charismatic former Nazi and creator of the German V-2 rocket program. In sum, do you believe his impact on the world was positive or negative? How about his predictions about the future of the U.S. Space Program?

The Day

This second section is dedicated to the events of one day - December 7th 1972. There is a mix of print and visual media, and it is presented chronologically throughout the day, so the day begins with the launch of Apollo 17 at 12:33AM and the CBS Radio News at 1AM.

The morning is represented by the arrival of two newspapers, the *New York Times* and the *Chicago Tribune* (which works, as they were both "morning" papers in 1972).

The morning game shows are represented by *The New Price is Right* and *What's My Line?* with their corresponding modules.

Since I like to have music on at lunch, the top five songs for the week will be presented at that "time."

More print media from the day of December 7th is presented "after lunch" with readings and modules from *Jet, Rolling Stone*, and *TV Guide*.

Late afternoon and early evening features a rerun of *I Love Lucy* and network news reports on the progress of Apollo 17. Random news of the day from the Associated Press, including the attempted assassination of Phillipine First Lady Imelda Marcos, Kissinger at the Peace Talks in Paris, and information on how to pick out a Christmas tree are also included.

A thorough coverage of the day is presented with the full broadcast of the *CBS Evening News* with Walter Cronkite. In this way, we can say "That's the way it is, December 7th 1972."

Musical interludes from evening shows are presented too, with Dean Martin singing "Evening in Roma" on his show and Deonne Warwick singing "Daydreamin'" on the Flip Wilson show.

Prime time television is part of the day too, with the *Mod Squad, Monty Python's Flying Circus*, and *The Waltons*.

The Day ends with *The Tonight Show with Johnny Carson*, with guests Bob Hope and Carol Burnett.

Thus, *The Day* begins with the Apollo 17 launch at Cape Kennedy in Florida and ends with Johnny Carson in California. One day from coast to coast and sea to shining sea.

Apollo 17 launch - 12:33AM

The only nighttime launch of a Saturn V rocket took place soon after midnight on December 7th 1972. There is one module associated with this footage.

Module 71: Thoughts

What are your thoughts as you watch the nighttime launch? The crowd who witnessed the last Apollo moon mission was estimated at 500,000 and observers in Miami reported seeing a "red streak" across the night sky. How would you have felt if you had witnessed the launch from Cape Kennedy on that dark night?

CBS Radio News - 1AM

Module 72: The news day begins

     Mitchell Krauss gives us an update on Apollo 17 and the condition of former President Harry Truman at 1AM. How do you think the 24-hour news channels have changed our ability to find out what is happening in the world? Do you see this constant news reporting as a positive or a negative?

The New York Times

"All the News That's Fit to Print"

LATE CITY EDITION

Weather: Clearing and cold today, quite cold tonight, fair tomorrow. Temp. range: today 25-35; Wed. 34-58. Full U.S. report on Page 106.

VOL. CXXII...No. 41,356

NEW YORK, THURSDAY, DECEMBER 7, 1972

15 CENTS

8 ARE DISMISSED FROM HIGH POSTS BY INTERIOR CHIEF

3 Assistant Secretaries and 2 Indian Bureau Officials Ousted in Shake-up

PARKS DIRECTOR IS OUT

Morton Is Also Expected to Make Further Changes in Lower-Level Jobs

By WILLIAM M. BLAIR
Special to The New York Times

WASHINGTON, Dec. 6—The Administration has ordered a housecleaning of top-echelon officials of the Department of the Interior.

Three Assistant Secretaries the two top officials of the Bureau of Indian Affairs, the director of the National Park Service, the Commissioner of Reclamation and the agency's mental adviser have been dismissed in the shake-up.

President Nixon and Secretary of the Interior Rogers C. B. Morton are expected to announce the dismissals soon along with widespread changes in lower-level posts, according to informed sources.

Continued on Page 62, Column 4

Truman on 'Critical' List; Heart Condition Weakens

Ex-President, 88, Rallies Slightly After Passing Through a Decisive Period in Battle Against Lung Congestion

By B. DRUMMOND AYRES Jr.
Special to The New York Times

KANSAS CITY, Mo., Thursday, Dec. 7—Former President Harry S. Truman's condition became critical last night, he rallied slightly about midnight as he struggled with a weakened heart to overcome an attack of lung congestion.

Mr. Truman, who is 88 years old, was put on the "critical" list at Research Hospital and Medical Center here after being listed in serious condition most of yesterday. He was critical Tuesday and listed as in fair condition.

At a briefing at 12:15 this morning, Eastern standard time, a hospital spokesman said that Mr. Truman had "passed through an ultra-critical period" about 8 o'clock last night.

A medical bulletin issued at 2 A.M. said that Mr. Truman's condition remained critical, although fluid in his lungs had "diminished." Dr. Wilson Miller, a consulting internist, also expained that he was "extremely"

Continued on Page 33, Column 4

U.S. PLANES STRIKE NEAR SAIGON BASE IN A REPRISAL RAID

Ground Pursuit of Vietcong Unit Also Reported After Rockets Hit Tansonnhut

By SYLVAN FOX
Special to The New York Times

SAIGON, South Vietnam, Thursday, Dec. 7—American planes struck tactical air strikes within 10 miles of Tansonnhut Airport last evening in an attempt to hit back at Vietcong forces that fired rockets into the huge Saigon air base earlier in the day.

Continued on Page 7, Column 1

Nixon Picks a Textile Man To Take Commerce Post

By LINDA CHARLTON
Special to The New York Times

WASHINGTON, Dec. 6—President Nixon announced today that Frederick B. Dent, a South Carolina textile manufacturer, would replace Peter G. Peterson as Secretary of Commerce.

Continued on Page 69, Column 3

REFUGEES TO GET U.S. AID PRIORITY

Postwar Plans for Indochina Stress Rehabilitation and Resettlement of Millions

By BERNARD GWERTZMAN
Special to The New York Times

WASHINGTON, Dec. 6—The Nixon Administration has begun postwar aid programs.

Continued on Page 3, Column 3

Truce Talks Resume

The Vietnam cease-fire talks between Henry A. Kissinger and Le Duc Tho resumed yesterday in Paris after a 24-hour pause.

Continued on Page 7, Column 1

GOVERNOR SCORES L.I.R.R. STRIKERS

Demands They End Walkout, but Bars Intervention—Talks Resume Briefly

By FRANK J. PRIAL

Governor Rockefeller yesterday assailed the 12 unions striking the Long Island Rail Road and demanded that their members return to work immediately.

APOLLO LAUNCHED ON FINAL FLIGHT TO MOON AFTER A 2½-HOUR DELAY CAUSED BY PROBLEMS WITH ROCKET

A FLASH IN NIGHT

Computer Signal Halts Countdown With 30 Seconds to Go

By JOHN NOBLE WILFORD
Special to The New York Times

CAPE KENNEDY, Fla., Thursday, Dec. 7—Apollo 17 blasted off toward the moon early today. Its fiery exhaust turning the night into day, in a delayed but spectacular beginning of the nation's last planned lunar mission.

The lift-off came at 12:33 A.M. after a delay of 2 hours 40 minutes because of pressurization problems in the third stage of the Saturn 5 rocket. A computer had halted the countdown at 9:53 last night, just 30 seconds before the engines reduced launching fire.

The Saturn 5 rocket carrying the Apollo 17 spacecraft lifting from the launching pad at 12:33 A.M., E.S.T.

Half-Million Spectators Wait in a Tense Silence

By BOYCE RENSBERGER
Special to The New York Times

CAPE KENNEDY, Fla., Thursday, Dec. 7—For more than eight hours it stood silent in the black Florida night, a brilliant white shaft, set shimmering by flood-lights.

Continued on Page 60, Column 1

Rackets Using Jersey Lottery Numbers

By RONALD SULLIVAN
Special to The New York Times

TRENTON, Dec. 6—The Superintendent of the state police testified here today that organized crime had begun taking the new daily New Jersey lottery as a means of determining the winning combination in the daily illegal numbers game in the state.

Continued on Page 56, Column 6

State Finds Quacks In Mental Therapy

By IVER PETERSON

A six-month investigation into the practices of unlicensed mental-health therapists by the State Attorney General, Louis J. Lefkowitz, has uncovered evidence of widespread "quackery," "sexual misconduct" and the deception of clients through the use of phony academic credentials and titles, it was reported yesterday.

Continued on Page 64, Column 1

An American airman, in flak jacket and helmet, taking cover in a building at Tansonnhut Airport, four miles from Saigon, during enemy attack yesterday morning.

NEWS INDEX

New York Times - December 7, 1972

Boasting the motto of "All the News That's Fit to Print," The *New York Times* began in 1851 as the *New-York Daily Times*; it became *The New-York Times* in 1857, and the hyphen wasn't dropped until 1891! The paper began publishing a Sunday edition in 1861 in order to provide information about the Civil War. Speaking of the Civil War, during the New York City draft riots of 1863, publisher Henry Raymond held the mobs back from the *New York Times* building (across from City Hall) with Gatling guns, one of which he manned himself!

To skip ahead a century, in the summer of 1971 the *NYT* published the Pentagon Papers, which were documents about the expansion of the war in Vietnam. Although the Nixon administration sued on the basis that that paper was publishing state secrets, the issue was settled by a 6-3 vote in the Supreme Court, with each of the nine justices writing separate opinions. Even they couldn't agree about all of the constitutionality arguments, but it was a win for the *New York Times*.

Our December 7, 1972 issue has no surprises about the news of the day - the Apollo 17 launch, Truman's sickness, and war news from Vietnam. There are four modules associated with this edition of the the *New York Times*. Complete any or all of them.

Module 73: Editorials

The *NYT* editorials are timely for both 1972 and today, dealing with issues such as the space program, the negotiations on the Vietnam War, the use of airbags in cars, and whether New York City was a good credit risk (the city nearly defaulted less than three years later). There's also a letter to the editor about marijuana! Which editorial (or letter) do you find to be most prescient about our world today? Why?

Module 74: Allende in the Soviet Union

The elected leader of Chile going to the Soviet Union for economic help was news in 1972. Less than a year later, Chile would be a very different place. Research what happened to Salvador Allende, Augusto Pinochet, and Chile in 1973. How is the country doing today?

Module 75: Polish youth

The Solidarity Movement was founded as a trade union in 1980, but the roots of it can be seen in 1972. From the perspective of today, why was communist "ideological training" likely to fail in Eastern European countries like Poland? What is the country like today?

Module 76: Land issues in the South

Mrs. Jenkins thought she owned her land. Then it was taken from her. This is a painful article about the struggle for fair dealing in business and commerce. Do you believe that this situation could happen today? Why or why not?

Chicago Tribune

THE WORLD'S GREATEST NEWSPAPER

Thursday, December 7, 1972

SPORTS FINAL ★★★★

Blazes thru Night Sky

Last Apollo Flashes Away

BULLETIN

CAPE KENNEDY, Fla., Dec. 7 [Thursday] [AP] — Apollo 17 early this morning blasted away from the earth's orbit after two revolutions and began its journey to the moon.

BY SPEED VALLARD

Saturn V roars off launch pad as last moon trip begins.

Half Million Gaze at Fiery Launch

Mixed Emotions on Last Mission

Page 4

Morton Begins Interior Shakeup

WASHINGTON, Dec. 6 [AP] —

Oil Executive to Volpe Post

Page 7

Turf Operator Aided Race Board Member Politically

BY RONALD KOZIOL
AND THOMAS POWERS

Tribune Charities Decision Lauded

Page 2

Board Adamant on Racing Dates

Power Ticket

List Truman Critically Ill; Family Near

KANSAS CITY, Mo., Dec. 6 [Thursday]—Former President Harry S. Truman, battling lung congestion and pneumonia, remained on the critical list early today but hospital officials said he had "passed thru an uneventful night."

Battle Flames in Cold

Called Gamblers Aid

New Jersey Lottery Hit

TRENTON, N.J., Dec. 6—

Weather

CHICAGO AND VICINITY:

Chicago Tribune - December 7, 1972

Founded in 1847 as the "World's Greatest Newspaper," the *Chicago Daily Tribune*, under the editorship of Joseph Medill was an early and avid supporter of Abraham Lincoln, the abolition of slavery, and the Republican Party. However, the paper is probably most famous for publishing the "Dewey Defeats Truman" banner headline in 1948, in which a smiling Harry Truman was photographed holding up the laughably wrong headline.

Although I was able to buy a December 7th 1972 copy of the *Tribune*, the first section of the paper was the only one available, which is unfortunate. While it confirms that the top stories of the day were about Apollo 17 and the health of former President Truman, it lacks any human interest stories. Therefore, there are only two modules associated with this edition of the *Tribune*. Complete either or both of them.

Module 77: Criticism of Apollo 17

Most media of the time were massive boosters of the space program, so it took some courage to publish an editorial which said "Never before had so many taxpayers spent so many billions, and so many thousands of talented technologists and scientists labored so hard on a civilian project that yielded so little." What do you think of Mr. Etzioni's criticisms? Has history proven him to be right, wrong, or somewhere in between?

Module 78: Vietnam Peace Pact

This editorial is interesting because it captures the opinions of Americans on the Vietnam Peace Pact through survey and polling research. How did the predictions turn out? Why do you think it is so difficult to make predictions?

78

The New Price is Right

The Price is Right originally ran as a daytime show on NBC (in 1956), but was so popular that it was moved to prime time until 1963. It has the distinction of being the first game show to be broadcast in color, and early on it was a Top 10 show. The ratings eventually declined and NBC dropped the show. It was picked up by ABC for the 1963 season, but was cancelled again as a prime time show in 1964, and as a daytime show in 1965.

The original version of the show was different in a number of ways from the later incarnation. First, it was hosted by Bill Cullen, who hosted 23 game shows over his long career (most famously, *To Tell the Truth*). Second, the show was run as more of an "auction" where contestants made bids on merchandise without going over the actual retail price! There was also an "at home" version where viewers would make bids on "prize packages" via postcard, with the winners announced on the show. Finally, each week had a "winner" (determined by dollar value of the merchandise won) who was invited back for the next week.

The Price is Right was relaunched on September 4, 1972 with the daily daytime version hosted by Bob Barker and a weekly evening version (which ran in syndication until 1980) hosted by Dennis James. Although Bill Cullen was considered as a host for the new version, Bob Barker was the host for the next 35 years. His last episode was June 15, 2007.

The daytime version was initially a half hour show, but was extended to a full hour on November 3, 1975. It was also renamed to just the original *The Price is Right* in June 1973.

This episode was taped in November 1972 and aired on December 8th 1972. I had considered adding a second episode that aired on December 13th 1972, but decided not to because a number of products, such as the Tappan refrigerator/freezer, Le Creuset cookware, and Glastron boat appear in both episodes. Years later, this repeat of products (a hallmark of the show) led to the most singular occurrence in game show history, when contestant Terry Kneiss guessed the exact value of his showcase on September 22, 2008. The story is a bit convoluted, but worth telling. Ted Slauson was a superfan of the show and had determined the exact prices of the items included in the showcases. That day he was seated next to Linda Kneiss (Terry's wife), who signaled Terry the exact value of the showcase - $23,743! Drew Carrey stopped the show and consulted with the producers and staff, who were concerned that cheating had occurred. The situation was sorted out, the end was reshot, and Terry and Linda were awarded the showcase.

In this section I have put the 1972 prices of the items up for bid, their inflation-adjusted prices (in 2018 dollars), and what they would cost today (if the products are still being made). It's an eye-opener!

The modules for this media are tied to the sections of the show (First item up for bid, Showcases, etc.) and include background information for the commercials and products on the show in order to provide some context for understanding television advertising and game shows in December 1972.

Module 79: Opening, first item up for bid, and pricing game #1!

Commercial 1 - Mazola Margarine

Inflation was an economic problem throughout the 1970s. Although the year-over-year inflation rate in December 1972 was a relatively tame 3.41%, it kicked into high gear for the next two years (8.71% in December 1973, and a further 12.34% in December 1974). To put this in context, the inflation rate from 2018-2019 was 1.8%.

With the rapidly increasing prices, people were looking for ways to save money, and the switch from butter to margarine seemed like an easy choice. In 1972, the argument for margarine was price and the "goodness of golden corn oil," but later it would be as a way to lower cholesterol. Until they discovered that margarine was full of trans-fats.

As for the naval "war-gaming" of butter and margarine, the commercial seems to be inspired by the 1970 film "Tora Tora Tora" which told the story of the Pearl Harbor attack from the Japanese perspective, and featured moving ship models around gridded tables to simulate their relative positions.

From Television City in Hollywood . . .

First item up for bid - Hardwick Range

The Hardwick Stove Company was started in Cleveland, Ohio by Bradley Hardwick in 1879! They originally made cast iron stoves, and during World War II switched over to airplane parts. While Bradley's son C. L. Hardwick retained ownership of the company until he died, it was acquired by Maytag in 1981.

> 1972 price - $476
> 2018 inflation-adjusted price - $2889
> Cost today - $650 or more

Pricing Game 1 - It's a new car!
Playing for 1973 Chevrolet Vega Sedan - manual transmission (specified!)

The Chevy Vega was a hit when it was introduced in 1971, and was the *Motor Trend* Car of the Year! Then the problems started: issues with engine vibration, rusting, reliability, safety, and engine durability. Critics felt that the car was rushed through production, which led to a number of recalls. One other interesting thing about the Vega (at least to me) is that it's launch was overseen by John DeLorean, who was a V.P. at General Motors at the time, and would go on to develop his own car, the DeLorean, which according to the documentary film *Back to the Future*, can be modified to travel through time.

> 1972 price - $2338
> 2018 inflation-adjusted price - $14,180
> Cost today - $15,000-$28,000 (modified on Autotrader), $1,500 as a "project car"

Game of True or False

Channel Master 8-track stereo (WITH a Multiplex AM/FM receiver)
      1972 price - $180
      2018 inflation-adjusted price - $1,092
      Cost today - $30 (vintage on eBay - tested to work)

Washington Forge 32-piece Town & Country tableware set
      1972 price - $35
      2018 inflation-adjusted price - $212
      Cost today - $99 (vintage on eBay - 58-piece set)

Since Brenda was correct, she is a "good girl"

Rival can opener and knife sharpener
      1972 price - $23
      2018 inflation-adjusted price - $139
      Cost today - $33 (vintage on eBay - tested to work)

Diamonair 2-carat simulated diamond earrings - "With the Spirit of Diamonds"
      1972 price - $120
      2018 inflation-adjusted price - $728
      Cost today - $22 (Cubic Zirconia)

      What is the biggest shocker for you when watching this section of *The New Price is Right*? Is it the change in prices? Bob Barker's paternalistic attitude? The clothes of the contestants?

Module 80: Second item up for bid and pricing game #2!

Commercial 2 - Flintstones Children's Vitamins
      What are the ethics of using cartoon characters to sell children's products? What if they're cartoon characters that were intended for adults?
      The Flintstones premiered as a cartoon version of *The Honeymooners* on ABC in 1960 in a Friday prime-time slot (8:30). While the cartoon was not a hit with adults, it was very popular with teens and children. The first two seasons were sponsored by Winston cigarettes, and both Fred and Wilma were featured as smoking in their advertising.
      In 1960 Miles Laboratory (who owned One-a-Day) developed the first "children's vitamin" called Chocks. In 1968, they created the Flintstones Children's Vitamins with different "flavors" and in the shape of various characters. However, there was no Betty vitamin (the excuse was that her waist was too thin) until 1994, when she replaced the car.
      Flintstones Children's Vitamins are still sold today in a number of permutations, and remain "10 million strong and growing"

Commercial 3 - Vaseline Intensive Care Bath Beads
      Vaseline was invented in 1872 by Robert Chesebrough as a "petroleum jelly." The

name was derived from water (in German, "vasser") and olive oil (in Greek, "elaion"). As for the history of putting things into bath water to help the skin, the earliest publications on this are from Japan, and are almost five thousand years old. Surprisingly, none of them mention Vaseline Intensive Care Bath Beads.

As a final note, a 2018 study published in the *British Medical Journal* (the *BMJ*, as it is known) found "no evidence of clinical benefit" of using bath oils, even in children with eczema.

Second item up for bid - Tappan Refrigerator and Freezer

Tappan was founded as the Ohio Valley Foundry Company in 1881 by W.J. Tappan. The company sold cast-iron stoves door-to-door, which is probably the best way to sell them!

1972 price - $350
2018 inflation-adjusted price - $2124
Cost today - $525 (for a same-sized Kenmore)

Pricing game 2 - TV and "burner base set"

Vivica is playing for a Spiegel color television and a Scheirich "burner base set." Although Spiegel was a famous mail-order company (and bought Eddie Bauer in 1988), it declared bankruptcy in the early 2000s, but still sends out catalogs.

1972 price - $1020
2018 inflation-adjusted price - $6191
Cost today - $129 (for a 32" television) and $35 for a burner base set (cabinets not included)

Shopping game
Vivica is referred to as a "bright girl"

Wishbone salad dressing
1972 price - 41 cents
2018 inflation-adjusted price - $2.49
Cost today - $1.85 (although they no longer make "California Onion")

Cornish game hen
1972 price - 89 cents
2018 inflation-adjusted price - $5.40
Cost today - $3 (although Checkerboard Farms no longer exist)

Lipton soup mix
1972 price - 39 cents
2018 inflation-adjusted price - $2.37
Cost today - $1.99

Holland House cocktail mix
This product doesn't exist anymore, but if you'd like to make a Grasshopper, it's

basically creme de menthe, creme de cacao, and creme shaken together in ice. It was a popular drink in the American South in the 1950s and 1960s (and apparently, 1972).

Royal strawberry gelatin
>1972 price - 19 cents
>2018 inflation-adjusted price - $1.15
>Cost today - 96 cents

It would be difficult to play this pricing game in 1972, but how do you think you would do using today's prices? Do you pay close attention to how much things cost when checking out at a store? Why or why not?

Module 81: Third item up for bid and pricing game #3!

Commercial 4 - Fantastik Cleaner
>"Dirt just disappears" when you use Fantastik! This spray cleaner was designed as a SC Johnson competitor for Clorox's Formula 409.

Commercial 5 - Shiseido facial mask
>Shiseido is the largest cosmetics company in Japan and one of the oldest in the world. It was founded by Arinobu Fukuhara in 1872, after he had travelled in the United States and Europe. He also introduced ice cream to Japan, which is interesting because most Japanese adults are lactose intolerant.
>The company still uses the same logo as they did in 1972.

Third item up for bid - Guild Grafonola Stereo Phonograph
>Although it is difficult to understand who the target market for this product was in 1972 (as opposed to 1922), apparently some people wanted a stereo that looked like a Victrola. I found exactly one (1) on ebay.
>1972 price - $277
>2018 inflation-adjusted price - $1,681
>Cost today - $199 (on eBay, although they list the delivery cost at $453.88)

Pricing game 3 - Gas grill, Washer/dryer, and "Men's" luggage
>Ken Adams, who was working as an engineer for the county of Los Angeles, still managed to visit *The New Price is Right* four (4) times in the two months it had been on the air.

Charmglow gas grill
>The Charmglow originally came with a lifetime warranty, and I found people online who were still using the same grill that they had installed in their Florida home in July 1966. So they were built to last in the town of Antioch, Illinois (pop. 14,430).
>1972 price - $312
>2018 inflation-adjusted price - $1,893

Cost today - $325

GE Americana Washer and Dryer
General Electric is still making washer and dryer sets, but unfortunately, no longer in that color.
1972 price -$467
2018 inflation-adjusted price - $2,834
Cost today - $529 apiece ($1058 total) - still GE brand

Skyway luggage - $248
This is a four-piece set of "men's" luggage from Skyway, which was started in 1910 by A.J. Kotkins as the Seattle Suitcase, Trunk, and Bag Company. His son Henry joined the business in 1936, and until 2012 the company was family-run and the largest privately-held luggage manufacturer in America.
Interestingly, they were the first company to introduce wheeled luggage in 1972, although the stuff on *The Price is Right* is conventional for 1972 and has to be carried around.
1972 price -$248
2018 inflation-adjusted price - $1,505
Cost today - $400 - (Skyway luggage sells for between $69 and $129/piece)

Ken is obviously a likeable contestant and it's nice to see him win! Which of the products he won do you think would be most useful in 1972? And what do you think makes the Skyway luggage particularly "men's" luggage?

Module 82: Showcases!

Commercial 6 - Nabisco Spoon Size Shredded Wheat
Shredded wheat cereal was invented in Denver by Henry Perky in 1890 after he saw someone mixing wheat with cream to help cure their indigestion. Perky developed a method of processing wheat into biscuits, and sold them to vegetarian restaurants. He built a factory in Niagara Falls, and although in 1906 the Kellogg brothers offered to buy his patents for making shredded wheat, he didn't sell until 1928, and then to the National Biscuit Company (Nabisco). It's interesting that the Kelloggs were even interested, as they thought that eating shredded wheat was like "eating a whisk broom."
Post owns the brand today (acquiring it through Kraft), and it is still marketed as a "natural" healthy alternative to other cereals.

Commercial 7 - Westinghouse Super Bulb
The "Arctic Night Test" was touted in Westinghouse advertising throughout 1972. They installed their 3,000-hour bulbs in "Eskimo" homes (the preferred term today would be Inuit or Yupik, as they never referred to themselves as "Eskimos"). The LED bulbs of today are expected to last up to 50,000 hours

Commercial 8 - Shake 'n Bake

Henry Hooper (Mrs. Hooper's husband) believes that the chicken tastes greasy! The solution? Shake 'n bake!

First introduced by General Foods in 1965, the commercials for Shake 'n Bake were popular because they often portrayed children "helping" to make dinner by shaking the chicken in a bag to cover it with bread crumbs and spices.

The brand is currently owned by Kraft.

Showcase #1

Home - Rath Ham, Dining room (Broyhill table, chairs, server), Wall paneling, La Creuset cookware, Sohmer piano - bid $2500- actual $2985

1972 price -$2985

2018 inflation-adjusted price - $18,118

Cost today - $5,714

Rath Ham (went out of business in 1984, but luckily, there are other canned ham brands) - $4

Dining room (Broyhill was sold in 1980) -

Table and chairs - $550 (on eBay)

China cabinet - $300 (on eBay)

Server - $550 (on eBay)

Masonite paneling - $150/box for wood paneling (2 boxes for 15 panels) - $300

La Creuset cookware - $1810

Sohmer piano - $2200 (on eBay)

Showcase #2

Fun - Doughboy swimming pool (18'), Glastron sport boat, ShoreLand'r trailer for boat - bid $2500 - actual $3520

1972 price -$3520

2018 inflation-adjusted price - $21,365

Cost today - $33,226

Glastron GT180 - $26,006

ShoreLand'r 1850 trailer - $3,999

Doughboy swimming pool (18') - $3,221

Which Showcase would you prefer to win? Why?

Module 83: Ken wins!

Commercial 9 - Hostess products

Actress Ann Blyth was popular in Hollywood musicals and was also nominated in 1945 for a Best Supporting Actress Oscar for the movie *Mildred Pierce*, but by the early 1970s she was selling Hostess Fruit Pies, Twinkies, and Big Wheels. The point of the commercial would seem to be that if this upper-middle class mother gives junk food to her kids occasionally, then I'm not a bad person for giving them to my kids. It's difficult to imagine Gweneth Paltrow making a commercial like this today.

Twinkies were invented on April 6, 1930 by James Dewar, who was a baker with the Continental Baking Company. His insight was that the machinery used to infuse strawberry shortcake was not used for anything when strawberries were out of season. The original filling was a banana cream, but when bananas were rationed during World War II, the filling was switched to a vanilla cream, which proved to be MUCH more popular. The banana cream filling was dropped until 2005, when it was reintroduced as a promotion for the film *King Kong*. It remains available today.

The Big Wheel was released by Hostess in 1967, and outside of East Coast markets was known as the Ding Dong, as it still is today. The reason for the name change is the confusion caused by a competing product which was also on the market, the Ring Ding (made by Drake's Cakes)! The name "Ding Dong" corresponded to a bell that was used in early advertising.

The fruit pie from 1972 is enormous, and all of the snack cakes were larger in 1972 than they are today. One way to date the commercial is by the absence of "Fruit Pie the Magician," who was the mascot of Hostess Fruit Pies from 1973 to 2006. His final trick was to disappear from the product labels and advertising.

Commercial 10 - Bronkaid Mist

One way to treat the symptoms of asthma in 1972 was through over-the-counter inhalers such as Bronkaid Mist and Primatene Mist. They used different active ingredients, with Bronkaid Mist using ephedrine and Primatene Mist using epinephrine, but the idea of a "fast-acting solution" to "open clogged air passages" was the same.

Primatene Mist lasted longer as a consumer product, but was removed from stores in 2011 because it relied on chlorofluorocarbons (CFCs) as a propellant and was therefore destroying the ozone layer.

But now it's back!

Primatene still uses epinephrine - it's just the propellant that's changed.

Commercial 11 - Avon calling!

Shopping with your Avon Lady is easy, relaxed, unhurried, uncrowded, and very friendly. Especially if you want to buy products from a door-to-door multi-level marketing company.

The first "Avon Lady" was Persis Foster Eames Albee, who met David McConnell (the founder of what would become Avon) when he came to her house as a door-to-door book salesman. He was using a homemade rose-scented perfume as a way to interest people in the books he was selling, but most customers were more interested in the perfume.

McConnell realized that "woman-to-woman" sales was an effective way to broaden the market for his perfume (and later cosmetics), and so Albee recruited other women to sell the products of the California Perfume Company. She trained 5,000 women as sales representatives in her 12 years with the company, and Avon eventually created "Albee Awards" for the best sales representatives.

There were 500,000 "Avon Ladies" in 1972.

Ken wins!

Commercial 12 - Stouffer's fresh frozen cupcakes
This commercial provides a number of scenarios under which Stouffer's fresh frozen cupcakes might be consumed. Stouffer's began as a dairy company (in 1898), added a restaurant component (in 1922), and then moved into frozen foods (in 1946). The company then expanded into hotels before being sold to a defense conglomerate (Litton Industries) in 1967.
The company was sold to Nestle in 1973.

What are your thoughts about *The New Price is Right*? How does it compare to the game shows on television today? Do you feel that the show represents a "simpler" time, or have things always been as complicated as they are now?

Module 84: The commercials
How do you think television advertising was different in 1972 than it is now? They were selling consumer products, but what else were they selling? Do you think that advertising has become more informative? Why or why not?

Module 85: The prices
What assessment would you make about the change in prices from 1972 to today? What types of products are cheaper? Which are more expensive? Why do you think that is?

What's My Line?

If you love celebrity panel shows, then *What's My Line* is for you! While it originally ran as a primetime show on CBS from 1950 to 1967, it enjoyed an afterlife as a daily syndicated show until 1975. It has had a number of subsequent revivals!

Today's show is interesting because of the celebrities. First, the panel. Soupy Sales was a children's television host most famous for receiving a trademark pie in the face at the end of his comedy sketches. Sherrye Henry (a Memphis belle, as Soupy introduces her) was a radio personality and author, as well as a prominent feminist and member of the Women's Liberation Movement. She was later appointed by President Bill Clinton to lead a part of the Small Business Administration devoted to female-owned businesses. Gene Shalit started out as "eternal teen" Dick Clark's press agent, but eventually became the movie critic for *The Today Show* from 1970 until his retirement in 2010. Finally, it wouldn't be *What's My Line* without Arlene Francis, who was a panelist from the second show in 1950 through the end of syndication in 1975.

The Mystery Guest, Patty Duke, had a long and distinguished career on Broadway and in Hollywood. In 1958, when she was twelve, she appeared on the game show *The $64,000 Question* and won $32,000! The next year she was on Broadway in her first starring role, playing Helen Keller in *The Miracle Worker*. However, in 1962, in a Senate investigation, it was revealed that *The $64,000 Question* had been rigged and she had been coached - she broke down crying while testifying before Congress. Since she had received the Academy Award for Best Supporting Actress that year for her portrayal of Keller in the film version of *The Miracle Worker*, there was no public fallout. After all, she was an actress!

The next year she had her own sitcom on ABC where she played identical cousins! When it was cancelled in 1966, she went back to movies, starring in an over-the-top performance as an alcoholic drug addict singer in *Valley of the Dolls*.

She mentions on the show that she had recently married John "Gomez Addams" Astin. It was her third marriage (although her second had only lasted 13 days), lasted over a decade, and produced several children. Patty Duke was also president of the Screen Actors Guild from 1985 to 1988!

While this episode was filmed in November 1972 and aired on December 13th 1972, I believe that the episode is indicative of game shows of the era, and so decided to include it in *The Day*.

This episode has three modules.

Module 86: Favorite celebrity

Panel shows are great because they can reveal who is able to "think on their feet" and who is inevitably lost. This is even more clear when the panel is made up of celebrities. Who is your favorite celebrity on this episode? Why?

Module 87: The cues and clues

Besides the ages of the celebrities, what are the clues that this game show was filmed five decades ago? Is it the way they are dressed? The hairstyles? The topics they discuss? Which, if any, or the people look and act like they could be from our own time?

Module 88: Offensiveness?

The show ends with everyone in Santa Claus costumes and host Larry Blyden exclaiming that "This is the year for Jewish Santa Claus." The camera then cuts to Soupy Sales, who grew up in the only Jewish family in a small North Carolina town - his father ran a store, and Soupy would joke that the Ku Klux Klan would come to buy their sheets for their costumes from his father. Gene Shalit was also Jewish. Blyden's joke was clearly acceptable in 1972 - would it be today? And was it even acceptable in 1972?

Top Music

Popular music is always a reflection of its time, and the first week of December 1972 was no exception. Here is some background on the songs that took up the top 5 slots in the Billboard Hot 100 for the week of December 7th. People of a certain age might want to read the following in the voice of Casey Kasem.

Topping the charts is the anthem of the Women's Liberation Movement, "I am Woman" by Helen Reddy. The song originally appeared on a 1971 album, but was re-released as a single in mid-1972, and then topped the charts by early December. Reddy, who co-wrote the song, said that she was looking to write a song about female empowerment, since songs like "I Feel Pretty" (from *West Side Story*) were all that was available to women at the time. She said that the words came to her as she lay in bed - "I am strong. I am invincible. I am woman," and wrote in her autobiography that for years after its release, she would receive letters from young women thanking her and crediting her for inspiring their decisions to go to college, law school, and professional careers.

Second on the chart (and an eventual #1) was "Papa Was a Rollin' Stone" by the Temptations. This Motown powerhouse recorded the song for their 1972 album *All Directions*, and they won three Grammy Awards for it. There was some controversy within the group over the lyrics, as they had to re-record them a number of times to get them right. Further, the lyric about "the third of September . . . the day my daddy died" was controversial because Temptations member Dennis Edwards father had died on the third of October. Norman Whitfield, who worked for Motown and wrote the song, refused to change the lyric.

Herold Melvin and the Blue Notes take the third position on the chart with their hit "If You Don't Know Me By Now." Released as a single in September 1972, the song peaked in the #3 position on the Billboard Hot 100. The song was originally written for Patti LaBelle, but she never recorded it.

The fourth position was taken by Johnny Nash's "I Can See Clearly Now," which was a monster hit in 1972, and has been subsequently covered by a number of artists, my personal favorite being the ironic Ray Charles release in 1978. The song had peaked at #1 on the Hot 100 in early November 1972, and was working its way back down the charts by early December.

The final position was taken by Al Green's "You Ought To be With Me," which peaked at #3 on the Hot 100 chart in late December.

Module 89: Favorite

This is completely a matter of personal choice, but which Top 5 song is your favorite? Do you have a memory tied to any of them? What is it?

Module 90: Aging well?

Which of the Top 5 songs do you believe has aged the best? Why? And which do you think is most indicative of the music scene in 1972?

Module 91: Clothes

After you watch the videos of the songs, which performers do you believe are wearing the most iconic "1972" clothes? Why? I have to say that my personal favorites are the jumpsuits worn by the Blue Notes. Or the hot pink tuxedos worn by the Temptations. Classic!

DEC. 7, 1972/35¢ A JOHNSON PUBLICATION

JET

**WHAT DOPE ARREST
IS DOING TO CAREER
OF BARBARA McNAIR**

Jet

The first issue of *Jet* appeared in 1951 with the intention of providing news about African-American culture and entertainment. Publisher John H. Johnson had started the monthly magazine *Ebony* in 1945, and based on its success, believed that there was a market for a weekly digest of stories too. The name *Jet* was thought to symbolize "Black and speed" according to Johnson.

Jet became a chronicle of the Civil Rights movement throughout the 1950s, and rose to national prominence when it published photos of the mutilated body of Emmett Till, a 14-year-old who was lynched in Mississippi after being accused of offending a white woman in her family's grocery store. His murderers were acquitted by an all-white jury in 1955. Since they didn't have to fear prosecution due to double jeopardy (where a person can't be tried twice for the same crime), Till's assailants admitted to the murder in an interview with *Look* magazine in 1956.

This week's cover features singer Barbara McNair, who rose to fame in 1958 with her debut single of "Till There Was You." She was arrested two months earlier for signing for a package that was delivered to her home. The package contained a shipment of heroin. She denied any knowledge of what was in the package and charges were dropped in 1973. However, her then third-husband Rick Manzie was charged with the crime. Manzie was later killed in their Las Vegas home, allegedly as a mafia hit. It's a complicated world.

Jet and *Ebony* were both eventually sold to a private equity firm with the death of publisher John H. Johnson, and *Jet* stopped publishing a print issue in 2014.

There are four modules associated with this edition of *Jet*. Complete any or all of them.

Module 92: The deaths of Smith and Brown
Denver Smith and Leonard Douglas Brown were killed during a student demonstration at Southern University, at the time the largest HBCU in the United States. According to *Jet*, "To many, it was the inevitable result of institutional racism." For this module, research how the situation developed and was resolved. Consider the way protests happen today. What has changed and what has stayed the same?

Module 93: Jesse Jackson works for dual citizenship in Liberia
As the article states, Liberia was founded as a homeland for Black freedmen from the United States. To this day, citizenship is granted by race, and only to people of Black African origin (although now, others can become permanent residents). What do you think of the idea of dual citizenship for African-Americans? For this module, research Liberia and the fate of President Tolbert.

Module 94: The dangers of testifying in a gang murder
How do you balance the responsibilities of being a witness to a murder with the concerns for the safety of your family? What would you do if you were in Mrs. Carradine's

place?

Module 95: Mixed marriages

Attitudes about interracial marriage have changed significantly since 1972. Or have they? Research the latest survey findings and compare them to the numbers reported in *Jet*. What would you conclude? What surprised you the most?

A Fifth Anniversary Issue Treat: Our Back Pages

IND 34145

ROLLING STONE

60¢
December 7, 1972
Issue No. 123
UK 20p

The Resurrection of Carlos Santana
by Ben Fong-Torres

The Strange Case of the Hippie Mafia
by Joe Eszterhas

The First Intergalactic Space War Olympics
by Stewart Brand

Your Friendly Federal Grand Juries: Farewell to the Fifth Amendment

Halloween Daze: Midnite at The Vice Palace

Rolling Stone

Rolling Stone came out with a first issue on November 9, 1967 in a biweekly newspaper format. At the time, Jann Wenner (one of the founders) said that the name came from Muddy Waters 1950s blues song "Rollin' Stone" and Bob Dylan's 1965 "Like a Rolling Stone," but of course they were also influenced by the group of the same name (although that admission didn't come out until years later).

Although it was started in the heart of the hippie counterculture movement of San Francisco, one of the goals of the magazine was to cover music in a more conventional, journalistic tradition. While most other music magazines of the time focussed on radical politics, *Rolling Stone* was able to attract writers like Hunter S. Thompson and Thomas Wolfe. In fact, at the time the December 7, 1972 edition came out, Wolfe was on assignment for the magazine to write an article about the Apollo 17 mission. His article came out in four parts in 1973 and was titled "Post-Orbital Remorse." It led to Wolfe's seven-year investigation into the space program, and finished with his classic book *The Right Stuff*.

Guitarist and songwriter Carlos Santana graces the cover of our issue. Formed in San Francisco in 1966, the band Santana was at a peak of popularity at the end of 1972, with their album *Santana III* reaching #1 on the Billboard 200 album chart the previous year. Their latest album, *Caravanserai*, debuted at #8 on the Billboard chart when it was released on October 11, 1972. When the cover article came out, the band was on a world-wide tour that would last until December 1973! THAT's a long tour.

Also in this issue (and included in a module) is an article on the "Hippie Mafia" by Joe Eszterhas. If his name seems familiar, it's because he went on to write the screenplays of a number of 1980s movies, including *Flashdance*, *Jagged Edge*, *Sliver*, and most famously, *Basic Instinct*. He also wrote *Showgirls* in 1995, effectively ending his screenwriting career, although the film eventually made over $100 million in rentals as a cult classic.

There are three modules associated with this edition of *Rolling Stone*. Complete any or all of them.

Module 96: Joe Biden and Jim Kerry

Two rising stars in the Democratic Party get a blurb in the World News Roundup section of this week's *Rolling Stone* - Joe Biden and Jim Kerry! We know how things turned out for them, but research what the early 1970s were like for their personal and professional lives.

Module 97: Hippie Mafia

This is a long-form article about the war on drugs (specifically LSD), Dr. Timothy Leary, the Brotherhood of Eternal Love, and the drug culture of the early 1970s. What are your thoughts about this piece of participatory journalism? How does it reflect or predict our world and the drug culture of today?

Module 98: Spacewar!

This is an eye-opening long-form article on the "hackers," "computer bums," and Spacewar gamers at the dawn of the computer age in Silicon Valley. What do you believe the impact of Spacewar was on later video games?

The article also discusses the role of ARPA (now DARPA) in the development of the internet (or at the time, the "ARPA Net"). Compare and contrast the "internet" of 1972 with what we have today? What uses are similar and what do you feel are the most important improvements?

Finally, the article discusses the future of personal computing as seen by the counterculture of 1972 - the year both Steve Jobs and Bill Gates graduated from high school. In what ways is the article prescient and what did the article get massively wrong?

15¢ Local Programs Dec. 2-8

TV GUIDE

On Location in Ireland:
A Risky Way
to Film a TV Movie
Page 8

Mike Douglas

TV Guide

While the first issue of *TeleVision Guide* appeared in 1948, the *TV Guide* format that became familiar to millions of Americans became a "national" publication on April 3, 1953. That first issue had Lucille Ball's new baby on the cover. Since it was only sold in ten cities, it wasn't quite a "national publication," but it quickly had a subscription base of over a million.

The schedules listed in *TV Guide* frequently contained a brief synopsis of the episode and special guest stars. Each channel was presented as a number in a round icon shaped like a television screen (as was the *TV Guide* logo). In addition to schedules, *TV Guide* contained feature articles on celebrities and "general interest" articles about the industry, and these are reflected in the modules below.

Our December 2-8 issue is from the Arkansas television market, but the pattern of listings for a weekday (December 7th 1972 was a Thursday) was pretty standard nationwide: game shows and movies in the morning, soap operas and syndicated reruns of older television shows in the afternoon, and network prime-time programs in the evening. Thanks to the synopses presented in *TV Guide*, I can replicate the exact episodes that were presented on December 7th!

There are three modules associated with this edition of *TV Guide*. Complete any or all of them.

Module 99: Rita Moreno

Rita Moreno became famous playing Anita in 1961's *West Side Story*, and won an Academy Award for the role. She also went on to win a Grammy, an Emmy, and a Tony. But in 1972 she was on *The Electric Company*, a children's television show. She took the role "Because on that show I represent all the Hispanic peoples in America." Do you feel that American television now more accurately represents minority populations? Why or why not?

Module 100: Mike Douglas

Singer and talk show host Mike Douglas was at the height of his popularity in 1972. Earlier in the year he had John Lennon and Yoko Ono as his guest hosts for a week of shows! He had an audience of 10 million and was making $2 million per year. For this module, after reading the article in *TV Guide* (and other research you choose), how would you account for such success from a daytime talk show host?

Module 101: So you need an audience . . .

Here's a job no one knew existed - audience wrangler. Near the end of the article, producer Chuck Barris (of *The Dating Game*, *The Newlywed Game*, and later *The Gong Show* fame) talks about why an audience wrangler is needed. Do you think his assessment is still correct today?

I Love Lucy

Supposedly, there was never a time when an episode of *I Love Lucy* wasn't playing on some television station, somewhere in the world, 24 hours per day, and this episode is further proof of that. Although it originally aired on November 19, 1956, since it was shown as a syndicated rerun on December 7th, I decided to include it in this project.

And I'm glad I did! "Deep-Sea Fishing" was part of a series of episodes where the gang goes down to Florida for a vacation. Desi Arnez had originally wanted them to travel to New Orleans, but the writers convinced him that Miami Beach (and later Havana) was the better choice. Desi had lived in Miami after leaving Cuba in 1934, and since he loved deep-sea fishing in real life (referred to as "dipsy" fishing the previous season), the location fit the plot.

A few other notes about this episode. The hotel where the gang stays is a real place, the Eden Roc Resort Miami Beach, and it is still in business today. Also, while they were originally going to use fake fish in the episode, it was decided that real fish would be funnier, and so two one-hundred pound tuna were purchased in San Francisco's Fisherman's Wharf and shipped in ice in child-sized coffins to Los Angeles. After they arrived and thawed, they started dripping blood, so the crew stuffed them with Kotex sanitary napkins. The show must go on!

Module 102: I Love Lucy?

No matter your age, you are likely to have an opinion on the *I Love Lucy* show. What do you feel were the best and least best (not to say "worst") parts of the show? How about this particular episode?

Module 103: Humor over time

Is humor timeless or is it context-dependent in a particular time and place? In other words, does hiding two dead fish to win a bet translate as funny over time? What are the changes you believe would be made to this episode if it were made today rather than in 1956?

Random television from the day

By scouring the internet I've managed to put together some clips of the day, which range from the mundane ("Picking out a Christmas tree"), to the historic ("Kissinger at the Paris Peace Talks"), to the horrific ("Assassination attempt on Imelda Marcos"). There's nothing to link them all together, so there's only one module for this media.

Module 104: Favorites

Which clip of the day is your favorite and which do you think you're most likely to remember? Why?

ABC News

Here's a small bit of news footage from December 7th 1972. I wanted to include this because of Harry Reasoner's commentary. The module follows.

Module 105: Harry Reasoner

In his commentary piece, Harry Reasoner discusses trying to cover the secret U.S. Navy Vanguard launch on December 6th 1957. Why do you think the government was so secretive about the Space Program at that time? As an answer to the Soviet Sputnik program, Vanguard was referred to as "Kaputnik!" Research the Vanguard program, the successes and failures, and what it led to!

CBS Evening News

While the *CBS Evening News* has technically been on television since July 1st 1941, there weren't a lot of viewers then because there weren't a lot of televisions. So we'll skip ahead to when Walter Cronkite took over as anchor on April 16, 1962. Under Cronkite the evening news went from 15 minutes to a full half hour. His coverage of the assassination of President Kennedy helped to make him, according to a Gallop poll, "the most trusted man in America." If Walter Cronkite said it, it must be true.

While the *CBS Evening News* switched to broadcasting in color in 1966, I'm afraid that our archival copy is in black and white. It's still a fascinating work of journalism and history, and comes complete with the commercials that were broadcast as a part of the program.

There are six modules associated with this media. Complete any or all of them.

Module 106: The Paris Peace talks

How is this evening's report on the Paris Peace talks similar and different from the print media's coverage of the same event? Which do you prefer - reading about it or watching a television report? Why?

In the statistics for the week, no American soldiers were killed and seven were wounded, while 1,247 Vietcong and North Vietnamese soldiers were reported killed. Do you believe that those numbers can be trusted? Why or why not?

Module 107: The Department of Transportation

I can't imagine a 5-minute segment on the appointment of a new Director of the Department of Transportation on any news program today. Why do you think CBS spent so much time on this story? What were the problems faced by the Department of Transportation in 1972? How are they different from the problems of today?

Module 108: Fire on board the U.S.S. Forrestal

This story slipped under the news radar, but Seaman Apprentice J. G. Allen was found guilty of arson and sabotage for a fire that caused millions of dollars in damage. While no one was hurt, Allen was also accused of distributing LSD aboard the ship. Research the earlier fire aboard the U.S.S. Forrestal involving the late Senator John McCain! Also research what happened to Seaman Apprentice J. G. Allen - spoiler alert: He escaped from prison!

Module 109: Commentary from Eric Sevareid

Known by admirers as "The Grey Eminence" and to critics as "Eric Severalsides," Eric Sevareid provided news commentary on CBS from 1964 until his retirement in 1977. His work won him Emmy and Peabody Awards. What do you think of his analysis of world diplomacy? Where was he correct and incorrect about the future? And what are your thoughts about having a "commentary" component on the nightly news?

Module 110: Commercials

Which was your favorite commercial? Are you going to start having cranberry cocktail for breakfast? Be concerned about your "irregularity?" What about the "saturated fat" when you're cooking salmon?! Apparently you don't need to worry about all of those triglycerides.

Module 111: Female and minority representation

Everyone we see on the *CBS Evening News* as an anchor or reporter is a white male. How do you think this altered or biased the news reporting in 1972? What kinds of stories were more likely to make it "on-air" and which were neglected? How does this compare to our own time?

Musical interludes

Through the time capsule that is the internet, I've managed to find musical clips from the December 7th 1972 variety shows of Dean Martin and Flip Wilson. The first features Dean Martin singing "Evening in Roma" on his show (with my apologies for the quality of the recording) and the other has banter between Dionne Warwick and Flip Wilson on his show before she sings her hit "Daydreamin'." There's a later module on the decline of variety shows, so this module focuses on the stars themselves.

Module 112: Dean Martin and Flip Wilson
Dean Martin had been a huge star since the 1950s, and Flip Wilson was the hottest comedian on television in 1972. What are their legacies today? What is each remembered for?

The Mod Squad

The Mod Squad was designed to bring the hip counterculture into the living rooms of everyday Americans. The tagline for the series, "One white, one black, one blonde," was meant to highlight the diversity of the major characters - three young misfits who worked with the police as unarmed undercover investigators as penance for their "criminal" past. The backstory of each was unique. The "white" character, Pete Cochran (played by Michael Cole) was a "long-haired hippie" who stole a car after being kicked out of his parents' Beverly Hills home. The "black" character, Lincoln Hayes (played by Clarence Williams III) had been arrested in the Watts riots of 1965. And the "blonde" character was Julie Barnes (played by Peggy Lipton), a teenage runaway who had been arrested for vagrancy. Together, they were the Mod Squad!

The series was created by Aaron Spelling, the producer who brought us *Charlie's Angels, Fantasy Island, The Love Boat, Dynasty*, and *Beverly Hills 90210*. But that was all in the future. At the time he was running a production company with *Make Room for Daddy's* Danny Thomas, although their collaboration ended when *The Mod Squad* was cancelled in 1973.

For the stars of the show, *The Mod Squad* became their career-defining roles. Michael Cole went as far as to title his 2018 autobiography *I Played the White Guy*. Clarence Williams III has also had a long television career, and is maybe better known to my generation as Prince's father in the 1984 movie *Purple Rain*. Peggy Lipton won a Best Actress Golden Globe for her work on *The Mod Squad* in 1970. She married superstar music producer Quincy Jones in 1974 and retired from acting to raise her two daughters. Although both went into acting, her younger daughter, Rashida Jones, is more famous for her work in *Parks and Recreation* and a number of movie roles.

Personally, I think that this episode is outstanding, mostly on the strength of the writing and the guest actors. Cathy Burns, who plays the "accident-prone" child star, was nominated for a Best Supporting Actress Oscar for her role in 1969's *Last Summer*. Although she reportedly hated the movie and her role in it, a number of critics, including Rex Reed, believed she deserved the Oscar which went to Goldie Hawn for the film *Cactus Flower*. The other major talent in this episode is a young Bob Balaban. Although he was in 1969's *Easy Rider* and 1970's *Catch-22*, he wasn't above doing television work, and also appeared in episodes of *Room 222* and *Love, American Style*. His decades-long career has increasingly moved into comedy, first in Christopher Guest movies (*Waiting for Guffman, Best in Show*, etc.) and more recently in Wes Anderson films (*Moonrise Kingdom, Grand Budapest Hotel*, and *Isle of Dogs*).

There are three modules associated with this episode of *The Mod Squad*. Complete any or all of them.

Module 113: Portrayal of the police

The idea behind *The Mod Squad* is that young, undercover, unarmed, "not quite" police can get into places and situations where regular police cannot. Based on this episode, does this premise seem to be true? And what exactly IS their role in policing?

120

They interview suspects, collect evidence, and live with potential victims of violent crime. Is any of this realistic?

Module 114: Is the show hip?
Premiering on television a year before *Easy Rider* made it to the theaters, *The Mod Squad* was an attempt to incorporate 1960's counterculture into mainstream American television. But is it "hip?" The authority figures all wear suits, but they're treated with respect. The "outcasts" are not just working within the "system," but they're working for the police! Is *The Mod Squad* hip?

SPOILER ALERT!
Module 115: Losing your trust fund
Another crime in this episode that goes uninvestigated is that of a financial advisor who loses all of their client's money without telling them about it until they have no other option than to "spill the beans." What would your reaction be to finding out that people you trusted had lost all of your money? How does this scenario compare with the actual experience of a number of child stars?

Monty Python's Flying Circus

Why limit ourselves to American television broadcast on December 7th when great shows were also being broadcast by the BBC? *Monty Python's Flying Circus* is too wonderful to pass up.

"The Cycling Tour" was the 34th episode of *Monty Python's Flying Circus* and was filmed on March 4th 1972, and aired December 7th. It is unique in several ways. First, it does not begin with the usual animated titles, but rather with Michael Palin serenely bicycling to classical music (it's actually a waltz from Act II of *Faust* by Charles Gounod). Second, it is the only episode in the entire Monty Python series that featured a linear story. They would usually just be a series of sketches. The episode was written by Michael Palin and Terry Jones as part of something else they were working on, but the group was running short of material in the third season, and so decided to shoot this material. Finally, Graham Chapman's adopted son (John Tomiczek) appears in a cameo. He is one of the children seeking an autograph from Irish singer Clodagh Rodgers. The other is Graham Chapman, dressed like a teenage girl.

There are three modules associated with this episode of *Monty Python's Flying Circus*. Complete any or all of them.

Module 116: Show vs. Movies

If you hate the humor of Monty Python, then this module is not for you. However, if you are a fan, how do you think that the show holds up versus the movies that they made? How about this particular episode?

Module 117: Offensiveness

The episode is controversial because it also involves "Yellowface," (people pretending to be Chinese in stereotypical ways for the purpose of humor) which can be painful to watch in our time. Do you think the comedy overcomes the offensiveness? Why or why not?

Module 118: Time vs. timelessness

Is humor timeless or is it context-dependent to a particular time and place? So many of the references in this episode are difficult for someone of our time - Trotsky is obscure enough, but Clodagh Rodgers?! Do you believe that this episode could be broadcast as new today or do you believe it is an artifact of it's time? Why or why not?

7PM
UNWANTED KIN THREATEN WALTON HOME!
Will the unexpected arrival of long-lost relatives disrupt the happiness of Waltons Mountain? Ralph Waite and Michael Learned star.

THE WALTONS

The Waltons

The Waltons was a new series in the Fall of 1972, and came into being due to the success of a television movie aired on December 19, 1971 called *The Homecoming: A Christmas Story*. The television movie, as well as the later series, were based on the book *Spencer's Mountain* by Earl Hamner. Ironically, the book had also been made into a 1963 movie of the same title starring Henry Fonda and Maureen O'Hara - proof that Hamner was an expert at reworking the same material over and over again. This ability served him well both in *The Waltons* and his follow-up hit *Falcon Crest*.

The Waltons portrays a close-knit family in rural Virginia during the Great Depression, and was based on Hamner's own life. He even provided the voice-over narration at the beginning and end of every episode. Hamner is depicted in the series as John-Boy and played by Richard Thomas, who has the distinction of being the only actor from the 1971 television movie who made the move to the 1972 weekly series.

The December 7th episode is titled "The Dust Bowl Cousins" and director Robert Butler won an award for Best Direction in a Dramatic Series from the Directors Guild of America for it. Butler went on to win two Emmy awards for his work (although they were for other series).

One other coincidence of note is that Richard Thomas (John-Boy) appeared in the 1969 film *Last Summer* with the guest star on *Mod Squad* Cathy Burns. Further proof that Hollywood is a small world.

Although *The Waltons* was often derided for it's wholesome stories and depiction of family life, it should be noted that the first season won a Peabody Award for excellence. The show was commended for evoking "a mood of nostalgia, of love, and of honesty." Further, *The Waltons* pulled "a piece of life, a portion of an era, back from the past for viewing in the present." I can't think of a higher accolade for a time travel experience.

There are two modules associated with this episode of *The Waltons*. Complete either or both of them.

Module 119: 1933 in 1972

You may notice that although the actors' clothes say "1933," their hair says "1972," especially for the men. Were there no barbers in Jefferson County? No men wore their hair that long in 1933, or even 1963! That's one of the reasons the Beatles were referred to as the "mop tops" and derided for their long hair. Yet every male on *The Waltons* has longer hair than John Lennon in 1964. That's one inaccuracy in the episode, but what others do you see?

Module 120: The ethics of petty theft

While the ad promoting the episode in *TV Guide* (to the left) appears to argue that the "unwanted kin" are going to "threaten" the Walton family, they're really only guilty of some petty theft because they lack money. After all, it's 1933 - the heart of the Depression! What are the ethics of theft when someone is broke, no social services are available from the government, and they are homeless and living out of their car? Do we interpret their actions differently in our time?

The Tonight Show with Johnny Carson

It would be impossible to overestimate the cultural impact of *The Tonight Show with Johnny Carson*. Millions of people tuned in for the monologue every night to get Johnny's take on the news of the day, and they could, because in 1972 the *Tonight Show* was on every day of the week, with Johnny Carson hosting during the week and reruns called *The Best of Carson* running on the weekends. It wasn't until 1974 that Carson was able to get the network to move the reruns to weekdays (so that he could take more days off), and that decision freed up the Saturday and Sunday night schedule. NBC's decision to grant Carson's request is why *Saturday Night Live* premiered in October, 1975.

The Tonight Show was the most profitable show on NBC in the early 1970s, and earned between $50-60 million dollars in profit for the network each year (which would be an inflation-adjusted $300-360 million/year). In other words, the show was a "cash-cow" for the network. It was also the highest-rated late night show by far, with a Nielsen rating between 7.5 and 7.9.

Others had tried to compete with Johnny Carson, with *The Merv Griffin Show* running on CBS (from August 1969 - February 1972) and *The Dick Cavett Show* on ABC (from January 1973 - December 1974), but they were unable to unseat Carson in the ratings. Griffin's show averaged a Nielsen rating of 4.5, and Cavett's averaged a 3.4, which earned Carson the nickname "The King of Late Night."

The year 1972 was important also because *The Tonight Show* had moved from it's New York base at 30 Rock to Burbank, California on May 1st 1972, and would make the move permanently in May 1973. The show still clocked in at 90 minutes, and wouldn't make the move to 60 minutes until September 1980. As another aside, shortening the *Tonight Show* expanded the time of *Tomorrow with Tom Snyder* to 90 minutes. When Snyder quit after a year and a half, Carson was given control of the time slot and premiered *Late Night with David Letterman* in February, 1982.

The December 7th 1972 episode was a good one! The guests include Bob Hope, Carol Burnett, Joe Flynn (from the show *McHale's Navy*), and Dr. William Nolan. I have taken the liberty to insert December 1972 commercials at the breaks (including the commercials that Carson introduces).

The modules for *The Tonight Show* (as was done earlier with *The New Price is Right*) are tied to the sections of the show (Monologue, At the Desk, etc.) and include background information for Johnny Carson's jokes, the guests, the commercials, and the cultural references in order to provide a deeper understanding of the era.

Module 121: Monologue

"Did you see the moonshot? Pete Rozelle had it blacked out."
This joke refers to the commissioner of the National Football League (Pete Rozelle) and the policy of not allowing television coverage of home games that are sold out. According to a *NYT* article from October 5th 1972, hearings were held in the Senate and the heads of ABC and CBS sports programming appeared and spoke against

hometown blackouts. So did the head of the Federal Communications Commission. Bowie Kuhn, who was the Commissioner of Baseball, also appeared because 10,000 Tigers fans showed up at the stadium when the game was blacked out locally. He also said baseball was in "good health."

Of course, blackouts still exist today, sometimes due to attendance issues (the NFL), and sometimes due to broadcast rights issues (MLB and the NHL).

"Last moonshot of the decade"

Of course, this was not just the last moonshot of the decade (Ed McMahon) or of the century (Johnny Carson), but ever.

"California courts doing away with nudity"

The Condor Club in San Francisco had the first topless (June 19, 1964) and bottomless (September 3,1969) entertainers in California. In mid-1972, the California Alcoholic Beverages Commission passed a statute that prohibited nude dancing in clubs that provided alcohol. This is the case that Johnny Carson is talking about.

Carol Doda (the dancer he mentions) was arrested numerous times for "lewd behavior" due to her nude dancing, and at one trial in 1967, explained why the movie *Guru You* was not pornography, but a satire of pornography. She was also famous for using silicone injections to increase her breast size. She had a total of 44 injections, and increased her bust size from a 34 to a 44.

Doda Dome, in Yosemite National Park, is named for her.

"Chicken soup and colds"

Lots of science and cultural references to untangle in this joke. First of all, the notion that chicken soup is good for colds has been studied for some time, and Johnny Carson was likely referencing a Wilson and Katz study from 1972. A review in the *NYT* in 2007 pointed to more recent research in *Chest* done by Stephen Renard at the University of Nebraska Medical Center. Dr. Renard found from blood samples of volunteers that the soup "inhibited the movement of neutrophilis" and helped with upper-respiratory symptoms.

Carson then uses this as a segue into making a "Jewish penicillin" joke and referencing both Linus Pauling and Golda Meir. Linus Pauling was a Nobel-prize winning physicist who was famous for advocating taking massive amounts of vitamin C, which was also thought to be helpful in dealing with colds (the research on this remains inconclusive). Golda Meir was the "strong-willed, straight-talking" Prime Minister of Israel from 1969 to 1974.

As a final note, Chicken Delight is a Canadian chain restaurant that in 1972 had a location in Los Angeles.

"In Dear Abby . . ."

Abigail van Buren was the pen name of Pauline Phillips, who started writing her advice column in 1956. Her twin sister, Eppie Landerer also wrote an advice column under the name of Ann Landers, which ran from 1955 to 2002. The competition between the two sisters led to years of estrangement between them.

The *Dear Abby* column is still in syndication, and is now written by her daughter. Ann Landers column ended with her death (in 2002), but her desk was purchased by advice columnist Dan Savage (he writes *Savage Love*).

"Possible merger of major utilities"

There was THE telephone company in 1972 - the Bell telephone system (AT&T - American Telephone & Telegraph). The conglomerate had a monopoly on telephone service in most of the US and Canada until it was broken up in 1984.

What Johnny Carson is referring to was a possible merger between PG&E (Pacific Gas & Electric) with Southern Pacific Communications (SPC), a rival communications company owned by the Southern Pacific Railroad. That company eventually became Sprint (an acronym for **S**outhern **P**acific **R**ailroad **I**nternal **N**etwork **T**elecommunications). The merger never happened, and there were lawsuits between AT&T and SPC throughout the 1970s.

"It's time to go back to New York!"

As mentioned earlier, the *Tonight Show* had just moved to California in May of 1972. The jokes which flopped with a Burbank audience which "doesn't read" might go over better with a New York audience which is better informed.

"Notice how the cruel ones always sit in the back?" - even Johnny Carson has to deal with hecklers.

Commercial 1 - Golden Star Ham

Armour & Company was founded by brothers in Chicago in 1867, and quickly grew to be one of the largest meat-packing companies in America. At the time this commercial ran, Armour was owned by the Greyhound bus company (also out of Chicago). Although Golden Star ham is no longer available, in a taste test held by the *Washington Post* in 1980, it finished second out of sixteen hams that were tested.

Armour still makes canned ham under the "Armour Star" label, and is currently owned by ConAgra Brands.

Commercial 2 - Vicks NyQuill

It started with Vick's Magic Croup Salve in 1906, and was changed to Vick's VapoRub in 1912, but it was the influenza pandemic of 1918-1919 that kicked sales into high gear - from $900k in 1918 to $2.9 million in 1919. The factory was forced to run 24 hours to keep up with the demand for VapoRub.

NyQuill was first test-marketed in 1966, and the name is derived from the idea of "nighttime tranquility." As of this writing, NyQuill comes in at least 15 forms, including Dayquill, Severe, VapoCool, and Cold & Flu.

This commercial is also selling the benefits of a happy marriage - someone who is kind, who cares about your health, and will care for you when you're sick. As the wife says, "I'm glad I married you." Her husband's response? "Me too."

NyQuill - Improving Marriages Since 1966.

What do you think of the quality of this monologue? Carson seems to think that he's bombing, but with a little background information, the jokes seem to work. Which joke do you believe is the most incisive?

Module 122: At the Desk

Part of the appeal of the *Tonight Show* was the banter at the desk between Ed McMahon and Johnny Carson, where they talk about their day. Carson shares his day of teasing a student driver, who after he teased her, was "done for the day."

Spin-offs
The first segment of this comedy piece requires some context so:
Felinni's Oxnard - Oxnard is a small city near Los Angeles - "a city whose favorite pasttime is eating a Pup n' Taco, drinking an Orange Julius, and getting sick in an Arco station."

Pup n' Taco was a privately-owned fast food restaurant chain headquartered in Long Beach, CA. Their menu had Mexican food, and for some reason, pastrami sandwiches and hot dogs. In 1972, they had 50 locations. The chain was bought by Taco Bell in 1984 primarily for their real estate - their prime locations all over southern California were ideal.

Orange Julius was started in Los Angeles in 1926 by Julius Freed. Originally it was just a stand that sold orange juice and "medicinal drinks" along with Bible tracts. The name came from people yelling "Give me an Orange, Julius!" The idea to add milk, vanilla, sugar, and ice came from Julius's landlord, who thought that the orange juice was too acidic for his stomach. The Orange Julius chain was bought by Dairy Queen in 1987.

An Arco station is simply a gas station.

Commercial 3 - Vicks Eucalyptus Cough Drops
Menthol cough drops are strong because of the combination of peppermint, eucalyptus, and other mint oils. Apparently early December is the height of cold and flu season - at least for advertisers.

The same product is still sold today as Vicks VapoDrops.

This section of the show is perhaps the most context-dependent in that it requires some knowledge of the eras movies, television, and consumer products. Which "spin-off" joke do you think translates best to our time?

Module 123: Bob Hope - first segment

It is apropos that Bob Hope is the first guest, as he was the most frequently appearing guest in the time that Johnny Carson was the host, with a whopping 131 appearances. Apparently he always had something to promote!

In December 1972 he was promoting his Christmas Special on NBC. Hope had a 60-year contract with NBC, which ended in 1996.

A few comments on his references:

Hope mentions working down in Red Foxx's junkyard - the show *Sanford and Son* was the second highest rated show on NBC at the time, with a 25.2 rating.

Hope talks about Phyllis Diller being on his show. Diller was an eccentric comedienne who did her first show at 37, and her initial two-week booking turned into an 88-week gig at The Purple Onion, which was a club in San Francisco. She said that she became a stand-up comic because she had a "sit-down husband."

Carson discusses the appearance of Hope in Albrecht Durer's "Adoration of the Trinity." The painting was completed in 1511, and offers documented archival proof that Bob Hope was a time traveller. It hangs in the Kunsthistorisches Museum in Vienna.

Hilariously, Hope claims paternity of Bing Crosby's children - "I'm responsible for most of his kids. Did you know that?" The explanation is that when they'd leave Paramount he would say "Have a good night." Hope and Crosby made seven "Road to . . ." movies together between 1940 and 1962.

Commercial 4 - Gaines Prime dog food

Gaines-burgers were a dog food that was shaped to look like a hamburger, but could be stored at room temperature. Introduced in 1961, they were enough of a hit that they were able to expand the brand into premium versions such as Gaines Prime.

The brand was discontinued in the 1990s.

Commercial 5 - Reynolds Wrap

The Reynolds Metals Company was founded in 1919 by the nephew of tobacco king R. J. Reynolds, and initially made foil for cigarettes and candies. Aluminum foil for packaging was originally made in 1926, but it wasn't until 1947 that Reynolds Wrap was introduced. Reynolds Plastic Wrap came out in 1962. As the commercial suggests, Reynolds advertised their wrap for decoration, gift wrapping, and even fashion!

The company was bought by Alcoa in 2000.

In watching this segment, what are your thoughts about Bob Hope? He was a huge star for decades, but not many of his movies are considered classics. Have you seen any of them? Also, does Carson blow Bob Hope's cover as a time traveller or is the resemblance just a coincidence?

Module 124: Bob Hope - second segment

Bob Hope discusses dedicating the Walter Propst Building at the Eisenhower Medical Center, which was built on 80 acres in Palm Springs donated by him and his wife. The hospital was built after Clarke Swanson (the president of Swanson foods, which originated the TV dinner) had a heart attack while playing golf with friends and was too far from the hospital in Palm Springs to be saved. Former President Eisenhower had a house and played golf nearby, and supported the hospital by lending his name to the project, although he died before the groundbreaking ceremony. Bob Hope raised $7.5 million for the project by underwriting $1,000/plate dinners for wealthy donors (so that every dollar donated would go to the hospital), and the doors of the hospital officially opened on December 21st 1971. The hospital remains one of the best in the U.S. and is located at 39000 Bob Hope Drive.

Hope also mentions Spiro Agnew, who was Vice President at the time. Agnew later resigned because he had been taking kickbacks as governor of Maryland, and continued to take them while Vice President. "He got as many votes as Nixon" is a reference to the election blowout of the previous month, where Nixon won 49 states and 520 electoral votes.

Continuing with politics, Johnny Carson brings up Jean Westwood, who was the Democratic Party chairman (she preferred the term to "chairwoman" or "chairperson") for the 1972 election. She was, in fact, fired later that month, after being in the position for only five months. She died in 1997.

Hope says that Sargeant Shriver deserves a lot of credit for being a late addition to the Democratic ticket. He became the Vice Presidential nominee after the original nominee, Thomas Eagleton, was removed from the ticket after it was revealed that he was hospitalized three times for "fatigue and nervous exhaustion" and had undergone shock treatment for depression. Shriver was married to Eunice Kennedy and helped to establish the Peace Corps during his brother-in-law's presidency.

Hope says that the Democratic Party was so broke that they hired Clifford Irving as a consultant. To explain, in 1972 Irving was supposedly going to publish a "as told to" autobiography of billionaire Howard Hughes. The problem was that Hughes said it was a hoax and that he was going to sue the publisher (McGraw-Hill) if the book was released. It turned out that Hughes was correct, and Irving went to prison for 17 months for fraud; however, he eventually wrote a movie about the experience (*The Hoax*) and while in prison gave up smoking and started weightlifting. So some good came from it.

I think it's a funny moment when Hope gets a genuine laugh from Carson by saying that he buys his wife Dolores gifts overseas at the PX. A PX is a "Post Exchange" in the military - basically, a military-run retail store.

Hope says that he is going to do a Christmas show in Vietnam. I've put some YouTube footage up with this module if you are interested in watching some of it!

In conclusion, Bob Hope prepares for his walk-off by discussing the Paris Peace Talks and praising the American soldiers serving in Vietnam. This allows him to leave to great applause. A true master of timing.

Commercial 6 - Scott's Liquid Gold

Lee Scott began making his own wood-restoring formula in Denver in the 1920s and sold it door-to-door, but it was one of his customers, Ida Goldstein, who bought the rights to the product in 1951 for $175. She thought it would be a good business opportunity for her three young sons. The oldest son, Jerry, mixed the formula in the family garage, and built the product into a national brand. He was the Chairman of the company until his death in 2000. His son Mark continues to run the company today, and Scott's Liquid Gold is still made in the same facility in Denver that Jerry Goldstein built in 1970.

Commercial 7 - Jeno's Pizza Rolls

Jeno Paulucci started out by creating the Chun King line of Chinese food in the

1940s, but after he sold it in 1966, he started Jeno's Inc. In 1968 he filled an egg roll with pizza ingredients and invented the pizza roll! He sold the company to Pillsbury for $135 million in 1985.

In 1993 they were rebranded as Totino's Pizza Rolls, and are still sold under that name.

In watching this segment, while much of the discussion is about politics, are you able to ascertain Bob Hope or Johnny Carson's political affiliations? Are you able to do it with a little research? Do you believe that either comedian would be able to tell political jokes in our political climate today? Why or why not?

Module 125: Carol Burnett - first segment

As Johnny Carson points out, in 1972 Carol Burnett was at the top of her game (although it could be argued that she always has been). Her show was routinely in the top 20 in the Nielsen ratings, and eventually won 25 Emmy awards.

Early on, Burnett congratulates Carson on his marriage. This was his third marriage, and he had just divorced his second wife earlier in the year (she received $6k/month in alimony until his death in 2005 - it probably seemed like a lot of money in 1972?). The third marriage was to model Joanna Holland. Interestingly, Carson announced at the 10th anniversary celebration of the show (September 30, 1972) that they had been secretly married that afternoon.

Carson brings up *The Garry Moore Show*, a variety show on CBS which Burnett was a part of from 1958-1961 (Carson seems to think they did skits together on the show in 1966-1967 - time flies). The show was on from 1958-1964, when Moore asked to take a vacation and left the show for two years!

They begin talking about *Once Upon a Mattress*, which aired on December 12th 1972. I've included a small bit from it along with this module. The musical marked Burnett's Broadway debut (May 11, 1959), and she was nominated for a Tony for her performance.

Carol Burnett talks of graduating from Hollywood High and going to UCLA. An interesting footnote to this: Burnett grew up very poor; so poor that one of the reasons her grandmother would take her to the movies as a child was to steal toilet paper from the bathroom. At her high school graduation, Burnett received an anonymous envelope with $50 in it, which allowed her to pay for her first year of college tuition.

Commercial 8 - Vanquish

Vanquish pain reliever has been available since 1964, but I haven't seen a commercial for it in decades. From a commercial standpoint, it would seem to have everything - Judd Hirsch (from *Taxi*, *Dear John*, and *NUMB3RS*), a catchy theme (the opening of Beethoven's 5th), and even a hand signal ("V" for Vanquish). It is a brand that is ripe for a revival, especially since it's still available in stores and online.

134

Commercial 9 - Calgon Bath Oil Beads
Do people take baths anymore? Who has that kind of time?
Calgon started as a water softener company in Pittsburgh in 1933, and by the 1960s it expanded to include a number of related businesses. The bath oil beads were part of the "bath and beauty" business division which was sold to Cody.
Calgon bath products were famous for the tagline "Calgon take me away!" Such are the healing powers of a bath.

What are your thoughts about Carol Burnett? Her influence in television was vast, and she had the last successful variety show on network prime time television. Why do you think it has been so difficult for anyone else to succeed with this format? Has the audience changed? Have the quality of the performers changed? The culture?

Module 126: Carol Burnett - second segment

Burnett's second segment begins with a pitch for her movie *Pete 'n' Tillie*, which came out December 17th 1972. The film co-starred Walter Matthau, and both he and Burnett were nominated for a Golden Globe award. The film was also nominated for two Academy Awards for writing, but won neither.
Burnett talks about her grandmother's relationship with a man many years her junior (he was in his 40s when her grandmother was 80). The apple didn't fall too far from the tree, as Burnett's third husband (drummer Brian Miller) is 23 years her junior.
Near the close, Johnny Carson says that Burnett's daughters are likely to live to "a ripe old age" and Burnett responds "I hope so." Tragically, her oldest daughter Carrie died at age 38 from a brain tumor.
So this was a busy time for Carol Burnett: hit TV show, musical, and movie opening - all in the same week.

Commercial 10 - Sansabelt slacks
The production values of this commercial are such that all of the money must have gone to pay pro golfer Tom Shaw for his endorsement.
Sansabelt slacks were invented in 1959 by Edward Singer and at the time were considered to be hip and modern because they didn't require a belt or suspenders. Dick Van Dyke wore them on his show! Although they're still available, the last of the "original" Sansabelt slacks were produced in the early 1990s.
As for Tom Shaw, he won four PGA tournaments before this commercial was shot, and then never won another. He was also the subject of some controversy about his age because after he turned 26, he just kept reporting that as his age to the PGA. For four years! When he applied to play on the PGA Seniors tour at 50 he was rejected because their records showed that he was only 46. He produced his birth certificate and was allowed to join. He currently plays on the Champions Tour.

Since all of the modules thus far have been about the celebrities, now that we're at 10 commercials, let's examine those. Which has been your favorite? Why? Would you buy the advertised product if it was available today?

Module 127: Joe Flynn

Like first guest Bob Hope, it's appropriate that Joe Flynn is on this episode of the *Tonight Show* because he made a dozen appearances on the show in 1972-73. He was famous for his role as "Old Leadbottom" on the ABC show *McHale's Navy* (1962-66).

Flynn talks to Burnett about working together on a Tim Conway special. This was a series in 1970 that was cancelled after 12 episodes.

Flynn also discusses attending the opening of Disney World on October 1, 1971. At the time, a single day ticket cost $3.50 (inflation adjusted - $21.94). Check out what a single day ticket costs today!

Carson asks about Flynn's unsuccessful run for the Ohio State Senate in 1950. Flynn ran as a Republican. After losing, he went out to Hollywood.

Near the end of the interview, Flynn says "I don't think the governor thinks that actors should be in public life." The governor of California at the time was, of course, Ronald Reagan.

Commercial 11 - Dubonnet

Farrah Fawcett in a cowboy hat! Dubonnet is a "fortified wine" that was invented in France in 1846. Perhaps the "little old lady" she is referring to is the Queen Mother, who preferred a 30% gin/70% Dubonnet with a slice of lemon under the ice. It was her favorite drink, and she once said before a trip, " I think I will take two small bottles of Dubonnet and gin with me this morning, in case it is needed."

The Dubonnet sold in America is 19% alcohol, so Tom Selleck (the guy in the video) won't need too much to get himself and Farrah Fawcett plastered.

Commercial 12 - Trouble aftershave

Perhaps no product is as much "of its time" as Trouble aftershave. It was Mennen's response to Hai Karate aftershave, which featured commercials where men who wore it would have to defend themselves from women who were driven mad by the scent.

Since the scent is supposed to last all day (10 hours!) "A little Trouble in the morning, and you've got Trouble all day."

Keeping with the theme of commercials, celebrities, and inappropriate behavior in advertising, what products (like cigarettes) do you believe will be banned for sale in the future? Which do you believe should be banned now?

Module 128: Dr. William Nolan - first and second segment

Although he is on the *Tonight Show* to promote his book *A Surgeon's World*, Dr. Nolan wrote a medical column for years in *McCall's* magazine, and was a debunker of the medical frauds of his time, including faith healing and psychic surgery.

136

Dr. Nolan talks about how difficult it is to get into medical school, and how rural areas are underserved by doctors (and surgeons). It's ironic how little has changed in the past 50 years in regard to both of those issues. He also talks about adding "an inch" to each side of an incision during surgery when he needs more room to work; he would have a difficult time in our era of minimally invasive surgery.

In the first segment, Carson brings up Dr. Max Jacobson, also known as "Miracle Max" or "Dr. Feelgood." He was an Upper East Side physician famous for giving his patients "miracle tissue regenerator" shots, which were basically drug cocktails primarily containing amphetamines and vitamins. His most famous patient was JFK, but he treated many of the most prominent celebrities of his time. Kennedy famously said about the injections, "I don't care if it's horse piss. It works." By the late 1960s Jacobson was taking enough amphetamines himself to stay awake for 24 hours a day! His medical license was revoked in 1975.

I've put the December 4th 1972 *New York Times* article that Carson refers to up as a part of this module if you would like to read it.

Commercial 13 - Kraft Peanut Brittle

Ostensibly this commercial is selling peanut brittle, but the main product seems to be gender role stereotypes. It features a little girl asking questions, and her father "mansplaining" the answers. I would also point out that he's doing woodworking in a collared shirt and a sweater.

The tagline "Thanks Mom." seals the point - provide unseen support (literally, in this case) to your family with the hope of eventual acknowledgment of the effort.

Commercial 14 - Mayflower

The idea of playing Central American rebellions for laughs comes from the 1971 Woody Allen movie *Bananas*, where he inadvertently becomes dictator of the country of San Marcos. The idea of a deposed dictator calling a moving company is absurdist brilliance, as is the final shot of the commercial. Clearly, some of the best creative people were working in Madison Avenue advertising firms in 1972.

Dr. William Nolan - second segment

Acupuncture remains a mystery. Dr. Nolan says that "if a man like James Reston is impressed by it, he's a knowledgeable fellow, and there's got to be something to it." Dr. Nolan is referring to a July 26, 1971 article in the *New York Times* where Reston describes having his appendix taken out by the surgeons at the "Anti-Imperialists Hospital" in Peking. I've put the article up as a part of this module if you would like to read it.

Near the end of the interview, Dr. Nolan talks about a neurosurgeon in New York City paying $8,000/year (inflation adjusted - $48, 557) in premiums for malpractice insurance. By 2005, the average premium across the United States for neurosurgeons was $100k/yr, and in some states the premium was over $300k!

In closing, Dr. Nolan passed away from heart disease in 1986.

Dr. Nolan, in my opinion, looks like a doctor from a 1970's medical television drama - straight out of central casting! He was clearly literate and concerned about the welfare of his patients. Do you believe that this stereotype remains in place for medical professionals today or do you think that the field has changed? Why or why not?

Module 129: Here's Johnny!

After watching the entire episode, why do you think that Johnny Carson became the "King of Late Night?" What qualities did he have which are exhibited in this episode that led to long-term success? What memories (if any) do you have about Johnny Carson?

Module 130: Yesterday and today

Building on the previous module, after watching the entire episode, compare and contrast late-night television shows from 1972 to today. How are they similar and how are they different? What aspects from each could be adapted to the other? And which do you prefer?

Debriefing

The third section is dedicated to reflecting on December 7th 1972. What have we learned about the day? What did the people of that time think was important? And how was that time similar and different from our own?

The *Debriefing* begins with print media which came out on December 8th (the *New York Daily News* and *Life* magazine) and December 9th (the *New Yorker*). I have also included news broadcasts about the progress of the Apollo 17 mission as it was happening. These provide us with more information about the week.

The news of late December 1972 is provided by editions of the *CBS Evening News* from December 25th (Christmas Day!) and December 26th 1972. In this way, we can see how issues from earlier in the month were resolved (or weren't resolved) and what new issues were rising to importance. I've also included the CBS Evening News from January 22nd 1973, as it was six weeks after December 7th, and a monumental news day.

While a number of documentaries are available about the Apollo 17 mission (and are easily found on YouTube), I believe that by far the best is *Last Man on the Moon*, which is the life story of Mission Commander Eugene Cernan. It covers the space program from the early days to its impact in our time through the story of one man. It provides an apt conclusion to the media provided in this time travel experience.

The *Debriefing* ends with questions about the time travel experience itself - favorites, reflections, and what has been learned.

Thousands See Mrs. Marcos Stabbed. Man with foot-long bolo knife lunges at Mrs. Imelda Marcos (right), first lady of the Philippines, in attack seen by thousands on TV from Manila yesterday. Mrs. Marcos needed 75 stitches, but survived. Assailant was killed on the spot.

New York Daily News - December 8, 1972

In order to understand the things that happened on December 7th 1972, it is important to consider what news from that day people thought was important enough to report in newspapers the next day. It has been said that journalism is the first draft of history, so the *Daily News* source provides us with that draft.

Founded in 1919 as the *Illustrated Daily News*, it was copied from the British tabloid the *Daily Mirror*, and was the first tabloid-style newspaper published in America. The slogan of "New York's Picture Newspaper" ran on the masthead from 1920 to 1991.

The *Daily News* has competed for decades with the *New York Post* for the most sensational headlines and covers, and the December 8th issue is no different, with a photograph of failed assassin Carlito Dimahilig wielding a knife in his attempt to kill Imelda Marcos, First Lady of the Philippines. She ended up getting 75 stitches from the attack, mostly on her arms and hands, since she covered her chest as he moved to attack her. Dimahilig was shot multiple times and killed at the scene, and his motives remain unclear. Mrs. Marcos felt that her survival gave her a "second lease on life."

There are five modules associated with this edition of the *Daily News*. Complete any or all of them.

Module 131: Genovese bust

Organized crime was all over the news in 1972, from *The Godfather* to the *Daily News*. How do the details of this article compare to the story about "Mr. Gribbs," Carmine Tramunti, the head of the Lucchese crime family, in *Playboy* magazine? What are the main businesses that organized crime was involved in by 1972?

Module 132: Home Alone!

While this story was probably not the inspiration for the *Home Alone* movies, a kid outwitting thieves is certainly part of the story. This is a good example of the kind of local, sensational stories the *Daily News* was known for - snappy writing / happy ending. What would you have done in a similar circumstance?

Module 133: Male feminists

Another great example of local reporting comes from the "Changing Consciousness and Conscience" forum held at The New School for Social Research. Consider panelist Laird Cummings and his explanation of the origins of male oppression - how is this argument the same or different from theories of male oppression today? Would you consider yourself to be a feminist (or "male feminist," as the article says) by moderator Alan Tripp's definition? Why or why not?

Module 134: The Reserve Clause

This is a module pretty much exclusively for baseball fans or people very interested in the history of labor unions in American sports. In 1972, the league minimum salary in baseball was $13,500, or an inflation-adjusted $83,661 (in 2019 dollars). As of

2020, the league minimum salary in baseball is $563,500. Players' union leader Marvin Miller knew what he was doing. After reading the article, research the "reserve clause" and the cases of Curt Flood in 1969 and Andy Messersmith and Dave McNally in 1975. Do you believe that baseball has changed for the better? And what does this story teach about the power of unionization?

Module 135: Comics

The "funny papers" used to be a standard section of any newspaper, but reading them today they don't seem as funny. Which is your favorite cartoon? Which cartoon did you enjoy as a child that is NOT in the Daily News? And why was it your favorite?

144

LIFE

DIANA ROSS

The star
shows off
home
husband
and
babies

A
U.S. pilot
gets through
his last mission
—and then home

The pocket
calculator
craze

DECEMBER 8 · 1972 · 50¢

Life - December 8, 1972

Diana Ross is featured on the December 8th cover, as her movie *Lady Sings the Blues* (loosely based on the life of Billie Holiday) opened in October. The movie was a hit, with Ross receiving a Golden Globe and an Academy Award nomination for Best Actress. The soundtrack to the movie was a success too, and reached the top position on the Billboard 200 chart.

But even with dying presidents and rising celebrities on the cover, *Life* magazine was not doing well, and December 29th 1972 would be the last weekly publication. Although the magazine was still popular, it was rapidly losing circulation, going from 8.5 million copies in January 1971 to 5.5 million in January 1972. Part of the problem was that the vast majority (96%) of circulation was due to subscriptions, while newsstand sales were more lucrative. Writing staff was cut considerably, and the magazine limped through 1972.

From 1972 through 1978, *Life* was published in ten special editions per year based on particular themes such as "The Year in Pictures." It made a comeback as a monthly in 1978, but ceased regular publication for good in May 2000. Special editions continue to come out periodically.

There are three modules for this edition of *Life*. Complete any or all of them.

Module 136: Pocket calculators!

I still remember when our house got its first "pocket calculator" that my dad brought home from work, and I still have (and use) the calculator that got me through all my college and graduate-level statistics classes. Research an "inflation calculator" to see what these technological marvels would cost in inflation-adjusted dollars. How has the declining price of technology impacted your life today?

Module 137: What IS "a woman's place?"

In order to understand how far we've come as a society, it's important to consider where we were in 1972. The case of Janet Bonnema illustrates how gender discrimination was used to keep women out of jobs, and how individuals fought back to challenge that system. How have expectations changed since 1972, and how have they remained the same? Is this story an artifact of 1972, or is it relevant today?

Module 138: Death of the old-school cop

Police work has never been easy. The police officers interviewed have fears of being "set up" by internal affairs investigators. Has police work changed since 1972? Are their fears still the same? How is policing different today?

The New Yorker - December 9, 1972

The New Yorker has always prided itself on journalistic sophistication, with founder Harold Ross declaring that it is "not edited for the old lady in Dubuque." And he would know, because he edited the weekly magazine from the inaugural issue of February 21st 1925 until his death in 1951. For our 1972 issue, *The New Yorker* was edited by William Shawn, who held the position from 1951 through his retirement in 1987. So there hasn't been much turnover at *The New Yorker*, and in terms of cover artwork, typography, and interior layout, changes have been minimal, even to our time.

Besides being known for long-form journalism and short stories, *The New Yorker* is known for single-panel cartoons. The cartoons are often very clever and have sometimes started catch phrases, most famously in 1941, where a man walking away from his crashed plane announces, 'Well, back to the old drawing board."

Our December 9th 1972 edition features cover art of an angel decorating the sky over New York by illustrator Charles E. Martin. He began working for *The New Yorker* in 1938 and contributed hundreds of covers and cartoons over the years. He passed away in 1995.

There are three modules associated with this edition of *The New Yorker*. Complete any or all of them.

Module 139: The cartoons

Which of the cartoons in this issue do you think is the funniest? Why? Which one most says "1972" to you?

Module 140: The advertisements

It's not just the writing that's sophisticated in *The New Yorker*, but the ads too! Which ad is your favorite, and why? Which ads do you think worked better in 1972 than today? What do these ads say about the typical reader of *The New Yorker*?

Module 141: John and Yoko

The long-form articles in *The New Yorker* are long, so I wanted to limit them to just one for these modules. This "Reporter at Large" piece is about the (literal) trials and tribulations that John Lennon and Yoko Ono were going through at the end of 1972. John was facing deportation, Yoko was involved in a custody suit, and they both were co-hosts of *The Mike Douglas Show* for a week in February 1972. What do you think of their portrayal in this article? Research how the deportation hearings worked out for John and Yoko.

Apollo 17 news coverage - December 11, 1972

Today is the day of the Apollo 17 moon landing! While the network news organizations had access to the radio chatter between Apollo 17 and Mission Control, they did not have television coverage of the moon landing and so had to rely on simulations, animations, and models to make it clear to viewers what was happening.

Apparently all the networks were preparing full-length programs on Apollo 17 at 11:30 that evening, when the astronauts would be walking on the moon, driving the moon buggy, and film coverage would be available.

There are two modules associated with this media. Complete both or neither of them.

Module 142: Simulation and animation

Due to the lack of actual footage, each network uses a combination of simulations and animations to describe what was occurring with Apollo 17. While none approach the special effects wizardry of *Star Wars* (released five years in the future, on May 25th 1977), which network do you think does the best job with the Apollo 17 moon landing? Why?

Module 143: The Challenger

The lunar module which brought astronauts Gene Cernan and Jack Schmitt to the moon was named the Challenger. NASA has had a tradition using names of previous ships (such as the Enterprise, the Constitution, and the Columbia) for their vehicles. The most famous Challenger was the space shuttle which exploded shortly after launching on January 28th 1986. For this module, think of what you know (or remember) about the Challenger. If you remember the explosion, where were you when you heard about it? What were you doing?

CBS Evening News - December 25, 1972

Apparently Walter Cronkite doesn't get to take Christmas Day off! It was a Monday in 1972, so perhaps he had his holiday celebrations over the previous weekend.

As with the previous editions of the *CBS Evening News*, this archival copy is in black and white. On the positive side, it comes complete with commercials!

There are five modules associated with this media. Complete any or all of them.

Module 144: Leslie Stahl

The December 7th *CBS Evening News* had no female or minority reporters, but on Christmas Day we get Leslie Stahl! She was hired from a Boston affiliate because of the Federal Communications Commission's decision that women needed to be hired in newsrooms as part of an affirmative action mandate. CBS News said the next reporter they hired would be a woman, and that woman was Leslie Stahl! In her book *Reporting Live*, she describes herself as part of the "Class of '72," which also included Connie Chung.

Stahl started with CBS News in June 1972, and since she had an apartment in the Watergate complex, she was given that story! She writes "That CBS let me, the newest hire, hold on to Watergate as an assignment was a measure of how unimportant the story seemed."

One other story from her early career. While covering the Nixon/McGovern election night returns on November 7th 1972, while every other reporter had their "on-air" chair marked with their name, her's just said "Female."

For this module, compare and contrast the role of women in the news media in 1972 and today. What do you see as the main changes?

Module 145: Captain Darrel Pyle

Terry Drinkwater presents an emotional story about Elaine Pyle and her son Phillip, the family of Captain Darrel Pyle, who was an American prisoner of war in North Vietnam. Research Captain Pyle to discover when he was reunited with his family, and then when they were broken apart again by his death.

Module 146: No unhappy owners!

Actor Leslie Nielsen was a character actor for years before his breakthrough as a comic performer in *Airplane* in 1980. It changed his entire career, and makes it difficult to take Ford's "No Unhappy Owners" campaign very seriously, especially since they had released the Ford Pinto (with the famous exploding gas tank) in 1971!

For this module, consider whether ANY company can issue a "No Unhappy Owners" pledge in our time. What company do you believe could? Why?

Module 147: Earthquake in Managua

After the story about the tragic earthquake in Managua (the capital of Nicaragua), Walter Cronkite announces the relief organizations that viewers can send money to if they wish to help. People are "discouraged from sending unsolicited goods directly to Nicaragua." Do you feel that people are more sophisticated now in targeting their charitable giving? Has the advent of the internet provided more information to people who want to help, or do you believe scams are as frequent (or more frequent) as they have ever been?

Module 148: The Troubles

There was a Christmas ceasefire in Belfast in 1972. It seems amazing to me to be typing that in our time. What are your thoughts about the conflict in Northern Ireland? Do you feel that CBS News provided a fair depiction of the people on both sides? Why or why not?

CBS Evening News - December 26, 1972

The death of former president Harry Truman dominates the evening news, and is a fitting bookend to the *Life* magazine Truman cover from December 1st 1972.

There are four modules associated with this media. Complete any or all of them.

Module 149: The death of President Truman

Since I have worked as a professor for several decades at Truman State University, I would feel remiss by not having a module addressing the passing of the 33rd President of the United States.

What are your feelings about Harry Truman? Cronkite covers some of the highlights of Truman's political career. What do you think about his decision to drop the atomic bombs on Japan? His surprise victory over Thomas Dewey in the 1948 presidential election? His decision to fire General MacArthur during the Korean War? The sign on his desk that said "The Buck Stops Here?"

Module 150: Bombing North Vietnam

After Christmas, the U.S. military returned to bombing North Vietnam, and apparently it took 50-60 surface-to-air (SAM) missiles to bring down an American plane. Since the Paris Peace Accords would be signed a month later, research the effect of the bombing campaign on negotiations.

Module 151: Miracle in the Andes

Walter Cronkite reveals that the Uruguayan rugby team rescued from an air crash in the Andes had resorted to cannibalism in order to stay alive. I've read several books and seen the fictionalized movies on this subject, and believe the story to be incredibly compelling. Research this amazing story of human survival.

Module 152: Commercials

As this news broadcast contains the original commercials, what do you think of them? Deep heating rubs? Acid indigestion? Having your dentures slip? Trouble getting to sleep occasionally? The temporary relief of arthritis pain? Graying hair? Common stomach distress from trapped gas? What demographic are these commercials targeted to? Has that changed over time?

CBS Evening News - January 22, 1973

Our final edition of the CBS Evening News comes six weeks after December 7th, and provides a preview of the issues that would dominate the early 1970s and questions which remain unresolved in our time.

This is beautiful archival footage (and in color!), featuring Walter Cronkite taking a call live while on air. THAT'S breaking news!

There are four modules associated with this media. Complete any or all of them.

Module 153: Roe v. Wade

The lead story is the bombshell 7-2 Supreme Court decision to strike down abortion laws in 46 states. What are your views on this issue? What do you think about the news coverage of the decision? Do you feel it is balanced? Why or why not?

Module 154: Paris Peace Talks

Henry Kissinger's arrival in Paris marked the conclusion of the Paris Peace Talks, which dominated the news from December 1972. The Paris Peace Accords would be signed five days later. Reporter Tom Fenton interviews South Vietnam's Foreign Minister Tran Van Lam. Grab a cup of coffee and research what happened to Tran Van Lam after the fall of Saigon in 1975.

Module 155: Death of LBJ

In one of the more "you are there!" incidents in CBS News history, Walter Cronkite takes a call live on air from LBJ's press secretary to announce that the former president is dead. One of the reasons I wanted to include this video is because although I was only six at the time, I remember this moment because I thought "the President" was dead. My parents explained to me that LBJ was an "ex-president" and not to worry. How do you think such an incident would be handled by the news media today? Why?

Module 156: Watergate

Lesley Stahl reports from the courtroom on what will become the biggest story of the early 1970s. What do you think of the questions asked by Judge Sirica and the responses he received from ex-FBI agent Alfred Baldwin?

Last Man on the Moon

The life story of Apollo 17 Mission Commander Eugene Cernan is told through this documentary from 2014. While I would recommend watching the documentary in its entirety if you have the time; I have just put up parts which are relevant to the Apollo 10 and Apollo 17 missions.

Module 157: Apollo

Cernan flew the lunar module on Apollo 10, the "dress rehearsal" mission for Apollo 11, which would land Neil Armstrong on the moon. This media highlights the emotional impact of the space program on the astronauts and their families. What are your thoughts as you watch this? Was the emotional cost worth the payoff? Is it a cost that you would be willing to pay?

Module 158: Apollo 17

This media covers Cernan's experiences on the moon, and concludes with his reflections on having travelled there. What are your thoughts about the space program? Should the U.S. have followed through with the planned ten Apollo missions to the moon? Were the billions of dollars spent on space exploration worth it?

Time Travel Simplified - Conclusions

Module 159: Favorites
Now that you've completed this time travel experience, what were your favorite modules? Which media was your favorite? Why?

Module 160: People
One of the paradoxes of time travel is that while we can return to our own time, the people we read and learn about have to remain in the past. Who made the biggest impression on you in this experience? Who would you like to bring to our time?

Module 161: Change
How has your experience of December 7th 1972 changed you? Has it changed how you see our present time? How has it changed how you see yourself fitting into the greater human experience?

Background Research

In the past decade, the field of psychology has become more interested in time travel. Not like travelling back to December 7th 1972, but something like it. Think about what you did yesterday. Maybe you went out to dinner in a restaurant. Where did you go? What did you have? Who was with you? Or think about your plans for this week. What's on your schedule? Where are you going to be? Who will be with you? Humans have a unique ability to think about the past and plan for the future which sets them apart from the rest of the animal kingdom. This is a process known as *mental time travel* or MTT.

Consider our human ancestors tracking a buffalo on the savannah. They were able to differentiate the hoof of a buffalo from that of an antelope or a zebra. They were also able to tell how "fresh" the print was, whether the buffalo was alone or part of a group, and whether it was healthy or injured. The hunter had to rely on their past experiences to recognize what animal the tracks belonged to and foresee (or as the literature puts it, "pre-live") a future of where the buffalo is going. Even without distance weapons like a bow or a spear, the buffalo could be killed by running it to exhaustion and bludgeoning it to death. Contrast this with the way that lions hunt their prey. A lion will walk right over the tracks of an animal without noticing them. They lack the ability to associate the hoofprint with the prey they are seeking. Instead, lions stalk their prey. They see them, sneak as close as they can, and then charge in order to pounce or knock the animal over. It's the "smash and grab" approach to hunting, and works because most of the prey animals are faster than the lion. This is also why female lions often work together when hunting. But it's very different from the way that humans hunt. Humans are able to hunt the buffalo without ever seeing the buffalo. They know where it has been, and can follow where it is going. Seeing the buffalo after tracking it lets the hunter know that they were correct. This ability to think in terms of the abstraction of "past" and "future" is crucial and determines whether everyone eats or goes hungry. Unlike our animal brethren, we are not trapped in an "eternal present," but can readily recall the past and make plans for the future.

Researchers have conducted studies where they randomly ping people throughout the day to ask about their thoughts and mood. They find that people are three times more likely to be thinking about the future than the past, and when they are thinking about the past, it is as a guide to what they should do in the future. Martin Seligman, one of the founders of the positive psychology movement, goes as far as to say that instead of being called *Homo sapiens* ("wise man"), humans should be referred to as *Homo prospectus*, because plans for the future tend to dominate our thinking.

But let's return to the past for a moment. How stable is it? Let's answer that question with another question: Have you ever been on a hot air balloon ride? This is the paradigm used by researchers Wade, Garry, Read, and Lindsay (2002) to implant false childhood memories in their college student participants. First, they contacted the students' parents in order to obtain family photos from when the student participants were young. They also confirmed with the parents that the student had never been on a hot air balloon ride.

The next step was to use Photoshop to manipulate a photograph to make it look like the student was on a hot air balloon ride with one of their parents when they were a child. The students were then shown this photo, along with three other "true" photos from their childhood. The researchers found that two weeks after looking at the four photos, half of the students were able to remember very specific details about the hot air balloon ride that they had never been on. Many expressed shock when told that the photo was a fake.

Pictures don't lie, except of course when they do.

Other cognitive research has shown that creating a narrative story of an event leads to remembering it better, so Garry and Wade (2005) followed up the original study three years later with a narrative component. In this study, some participants saw the fake picture of themselves on a balloon ride, while others read a detailed narrative story about it. Again, after two weeks, half of the study participants who saw the picture of the balloon ride thought that they had been on a balloon ride as a child; however, 80% of the study participants who read the narrative story believed that they had been on a balloon ride. Why? The researchers believe that in a picture, all of the relevant details can be seen, but in a narrative story, the participants generate their own details about the balloon ride.

So how does all of this relate to creating a time travel experience through the methodology of Time Travel Simplified? First, there is no false implantation of memories - everything that you read about in this book actually happened on or around December 7th 1972. It is mental time travel that allows you to know that 1972 is in the past. Writing out the modules (or even just thinking about them) provides a narrative structure for your critical analysis of the issues of December 7th 1972. Most of the modules ask for your opinion on the material or how it relates to our own time. This act creates a narrative structure for your interaction with the historical past. You don't need to see Photoshopped pictures of yourself at the Paris Peace Talks to understand what happened there! Studies by a number of researchers (Grysman & Hudson, 2010; McLean & Pratt, 2006; Pasupathi, Mansour, & Brubaker, 2007) have shown that "by narrating the personal past and relating it to the present and future self [through mental time travel], people succeed to integrate changes in life and of personality across time" (Köber & Habermas, 2017, p. 608). In other words, what the Time Travel Simplified methodology does is create an understanding of a specific moment in the historical past, and relates it to the present (and future) self, allowing us to integrate that information into our life and our personality. As I wrote in the introduction, the real paradox of time travel is not that it changes the past - it's that it changes you in the present (and the future). After completing all of the modules, not only do you understand the past, you understand how we got to this particular present, and most importantly, you understand yourself - your hopes, fears, biases, influences, and ways of seeing the world - in an entirely new way. Time travel, at its core, is about human potential and personal growth.

I believe that the best analogy for the changes created by Time Travel Simplified is a "study abroad" experience. In both experiences you are taken out of your usual time and place and put in a foreign country where you have to understand how "they do things differently there" (to paraphrase the L.P. Hartley quote which begins this book). And the benefits of both experiences are very much the same. They both let us "see the world," whether it is a different culture in our own time or our own culture in an earlier time. They both provide an education in a new culture, allowing us to understand what is acceptable and what issues are important. They both allow us to discover new interests that can be pursued after returning from the experience. They both provide a shared experience with people who have gone through the same thing - we're now all a part of a Society of Time Travelers! Both experiences provide the opportunity for personal growth, allowing us to examine our beliefs in a new light through a different context. Finally, both provide a life experience like none other.

This book, and the series that it is a part of, are the culmination of research which I've been conducting over the past few years. What I have attempted to accomplish is the creation of a time travel experience that anyone can be a part of, no matter their age or knowledge of history.

That's why I'm willing to guarantee that "It's time travel or it's free." Why would you know SO MUCH about one particular day from the past if you hadn't been there before? And you HAVE! Six months from now the memories you've formed from this experience will integrate with the knowledge you already have and become a memory from your personal past, like a study abroad experience.

So about that guarantee. If you have purchased the book, completed all of the modules, waited six months, and don't feel that you have experienced what it would be like to time travel, then I am happy to reimburse you. The details for reimbursement are available on timetravelsimplified.com.

I stand by the methodology I've developed with Time Travel Simplified because I know that it works and has changed me for the better. I sincerely hope that you have enjoyed the experience too. Thank you for joining me on this journey!

Research References

Bluck, S., Alea, N., & Ali, S. (2014). Remembering the historical roots of remembering the personal past. *Applied Cognitive Psychology*, *28*, 290-300. http://doi.org/fpjk

Brewin, C. R., & Andrews, B. (2017). Creating memories for false autobiographical events in childhood: A systematic review. *Applied Cognitive Psychology*, *31*, 2-23. http://doi.org/dtb5

Corballis, M. C. (2013). Wandering tales: Evolutionary origins of mental time travel and language. *Frontiers in Psychology*, *4*, 1-8.

Garry, M., & Gerrie, M. P. (2005). When photographs create false memories. *Current Directions in Psychological Science*, *14*(6), 321-325.

Garry, M., & Wade, K. A. (2005). Actually, a picture is worth less than 45 words: Narratives produce more false memories than photographs do. *Psychonomic Bulletin and Review*, *12*(2), 359-366.

Grysman, A., & Hudson, J. A. (2010). Abstracting and extracting: Causal coherence and the development of the life story. *Memory*, *18*(6), 565-580.

Hardt, R. (2018). Storytelling agents: Why narrative rather than mental time travel is fundamental. *Phenomenology and the Cognitive Sciences*, *17*, 535-554. http://doi.org/dtb3

Hessen-Kayfitz, J., Scoboria, A., & Nespoli, K. (2017). The labeling of photos when suggesting false childhood events can enhance or suppress false memory formation. *Psychology of Consciousness: Theory, Research, and Practice*, *4*(3), 288-297.

Köber, C., & Habermas, T. (2017). How stable is the personal past? Stability of most important autobiographical memories and life narratives across eight years in a life span sample. *Journal of Personality and Social Psychology, 113*(4), 608-626.

Liester, M. B., & Sullivan, E. E. (2019). A review of epigenetics in human consciousness. *Cogent Psychology, 6*, 1-29.

McAdams, D. P. (2001). The psychology of life stories. *Review of General Psychology, 5*(2), 100-122.

McLean, K. C., & Pratt, M. W. (2006). Life's little (and big) lessons: Identity statuses and meaning-making in the turning point narratives of emerging adults. *Developmental Psychology, 42*(4), 714-722.

Otgaar, H., Scororia, A., & Smeets, T. (2013). Experimentally evoking nonbelieved memories for childhood events. *Journal of Experimental Psychology: Learning, Memory, and Cognition*, 39(3), 717-730.

Pasupathi, M., Mansour, E., & Brubaker, J. (2007). Developing a life story: Constructing relations between self and experience in autobiographical narratives. *Human Development, 50*(2-3) 85-110. http://doi.org/dxc2dr

Pezdek, K. & Blandon-Gitlin, I. (2017). It is just harder to construct memories for false autobiographical events. *Applied Cognitive Psychology, 31*, 42-44.

Rasmussen, K. W., & Berntsen, D. (2014). "I can see clearly now": The effect of cue imageability on mental time travel. *Memory & Cognition, 42*(7), 1063-1075.

Sanson, M., Newman, E. J., & Garry, M. (2018). The characteristics of directive future experiences and directive memories. *Psychology of Consciousness: Theory, Research, and Practice, 5*(3), 278-294.

Scoboria, A., Wysman, L., & Otgaar, H. (2012). Credible suggestions affect false autobiographical beliefs. *Memory, 20*(3), 429-442.

Seligman, M. E., & Roepke, A. M. (2016). Prospection gone awry: Depression. In M. E. Seligman, P. Railton, R. F. Butler, & C. Sripada (Eds.), *Homo prospectus* (pp. 281-304). Oxford University Press.

Seligman, M. E., & Tierney, J. (2017, May 19). We aren't built to live in the moment. *The New York Times*, https://www.nytimes.com/2017/05/19/opinion/sunday/why-the-future-is-always-on-your-mind.html

Storm, B. C., & Jobe, T. A. (2012). Remembering the past and imagining the future: Examining the consequences of mental time travel on memory. *Memory, 20*(3), 224-235.

Wade, K. A., Garry, M., Read, J. D., & Lindsay, D. S. (2002). A picture is worth a thousand lies: Using false photographs to create false childhood memories. *Psychonomic Bulletin & Review, 9*, 597-603.

One Last Thing . . .

I want to thank you for buying this book and participating in this time travel experience. If you enjoyed it, I would appreciate you leaving positive feedback in whatever venue that you choose. Your experience will help others make a decision on whether to choose this book, so feedback is important.

If you would like to support my research on time travel, there are at least two ways that you can help. First, I have a Patreon account for Time Travel Simplified which allows you to financially support my work and in turn receive additional print and video media with their corresponding modules. It's also an easy way to interact with me on what you'd like to see and to find out what I'm working on. Second, if you are interested in participating in psychological research about time travel, then contact me at my Truman State University email. I'm easy to find online - I'm the Mark Hatala who is a college professor, and NOT the one who is the dentist or the golf pro.

I will close by saying that if you are able to physically travel back through time to December 7th 1972, please visit me at my childhood home at 6297 Denison Blvd., Parma Heights, Ohio. My parents are Paul and Dorothy. They are good people and will welcome you. Their phone number is 216-885-0165, but you don't need to call before you stop by. If it is a school day, you can find me at Pearl Road School. See you then!

168

MORNING

5:55 **8** PASTOR'S STUDY
6:00 **8** GOOD MORNING ARK-LA-MISS
6:20 **12** SUNRISE SEMESTER
Law and Morality: Responses to civil disobedience.
6:30 **6** TEXARKANA COLLEGE
7 WORLD TOMORROW
11 SUNRISE SEMESTER
See 6:20 A.M. Ch. 12.
6:45 **4** RFD—Devotions
6 RFD "6"—Agriculture
6:50 **12** YOUR PASTOR
6:55 **3** **4** **10** DEVOTIONAL
7:00 **3** COLORFUL WORLD
4 **6** **10** TODAY
Apollo 17 progress reports are scheduled. Also: a display of Christmas toys; art critic Brian O'Doherty. Frank McGee is host. (2 hrs.)
7 COUNTRY MUSIC TIME
8 **11** **12** CBS NEWS—Hart
7:25 **11** ARKANSAS A.M.
7:30 **3** CARTOON FRIENDS
8:00 **3** MOVIE—Adventure (BW)
"Across the Pacific." (1942) The time is just before World War II. Dishonorably discharged from the Army, a captain boards a Japanese freighter. Humphrey Bogart, Mary Astor, Sydney Greenstreet. (1 hr., 50 min.
7 NEW ZOO REVUE
8 **11** **12** CAPTAIN KANGAROO
"Do You Love Someone?" a story by Joan Walsh Anglund. (60 min.)
8:30 **7** ARKANSAS: THURSDAY
9:00 **4** **6** **10** DINAH SHORE
Archbishop Fulton J. Sheen offers his views on Christmas cards.
7 MOVIE—Western (BW)
"Escape from Red Rock" (1958) After committing a bank robbery, a young man flees to Apache territory. Brian Donlevy, Gary Murray. (90 min.)
8 **11** JOKER'S WILD—Game
12 SESAME STREET
9:30 **4** **6** **10** CONCENTRATION
8 **11** PRICE IS RIGHT
9:50 **3** LUCILLE RIVERS—Sewing
10:00 **3** SPLIT SECOND—Game
4 **6** **10** SALE OF THE CENTURY
8 **11** **12** GAMBIT—Game
10:30 **3** **7** **10** BEWITCHED

Thursday

MORNING-AFTERNOON

4 **6** HOLLYWOOD SQUARES
8 **11** **12** LOVE OF LIFE
11:00 **3** **7** **10** PASSWORD
Elizabeth Montgomery, Bert Convy.
4 **6** JEOPARDY—Game
8 **11** **12** WHERE THE HEART IS
11:25 **8** NEWS
11 **12** CBS NEWS—Edwards
11:30 **3** NEWS
4 **6** WHO, WHAT OR WHERE—Game
7 **10** SPLIT SECOND—Game
8 **11** **12** SEARCH FOR TOMORROW
11:55 **4** **6** NBC NEWS—Kalber

AFTERNOON

12:00 **3** **7** **10** ALL MY CHILDREN
4 LITTLE ROCK TODAY
6 **8** **12** NEWS
11 EYE ON ARKANSAS
12:05 **8** LUCILLE RIVERS—Sewing
12:15 **8** OPEN HOUSE—Swift
12:30 **3** **7** **10** ABC's AFTERNOON PLAYBREAK
Special: "This Child Is Mine." A courtroom melodrama about a custody battle between a child's natural and foster mother, played by soap opera stars Rosemary Prinz ("All My Children") and Robin Strasser ("Another World"). A series pilot, written by Richard Deroy. (90 min.)
Cast
Elizabeth Thatcher . . Rosemary Prinz
Shelley Carr . . . . Robin Strasser
Martin Thatcher . . . . . . Don Galloway
Mike Rooman . . . . Stephen Young
Judge Hendrick . . . . Marjorie Lord
John Rodman . . . . James Craig
Jay Lawrence . . . . John Conte
Max Dettman . . . . Milt Kamen
6 THREE ON A MATCH—Game
8 **11** **12** AS THE WORLD TURNS
12:50 **4** LUCILLE RIVERS—Sewing
1:00 **4** **6** DAYS OF OUR LIVES
8 **11** **12** GUIDING LIGHT
1:30 **4** **6** DOCTORS
8 **11** **12** EDGE OF NIGHT
2:00 **3** **7** **10** GENERAL HOSPITAL
4 **6** ANOTHER WORLD
8 **11** **12** LOVE IS A MANY SPLENDORED THING
2:30 **3** **7** **10** ONE LIFE TO LIVE

Thursday
AFTERNOON

3:00

4 6 RETURN TO PEYTON PLACE

8 11 12 SECRET STORM

3 7 10 LOVE, AMERICAN STYLE
Mary Ann Mobley as a wife jealous of hubby's hot new sports car.

4 MERV GRIFFIN
Totie Fields and Dr. Robert Atkins ("The Diet Revolution"). Mort Lindsey orchestra. (60 min.)

6 SOMERSET

8 12 FAMILY AFFAIR
French's Old West vacation becomes a real family affair.

11 VIRGINIAN
The Virginian tries to free Elizabeth from an outlaw who has an old score to settle. Virginian: James Drury. Harge: Charles Bronson. Elizabeth: Sara Lane. Eva: Mirian Colon. Grainger: Charles Bickford. (90 min.)

3:30

3 MOVIE—Drama BW
"The Fighting 69th." (1940) The story of a famous regiment of World War I, beginning with the time of its training at Camp Mills. James Cagney, Pat O'Brien, George Brent, Jeffrey Lynn, Dennis Morgan. (90 min.)

6 MUNSTERS
Herman, stricken with amnesia, is taken into protective custody by the police. Herman: Fred Gwynne. Lily: Yvonne DeCarlo. Grandpa: Al Lewis. Marilyn: Pat Priest.

7 BOZO'S BIG TOP

8 VIRGINIAN
An aging dance-hall queen asks Judge Garth to help clear the name of her son, who was hanged for murder by vigilantes. Rosanna Dobie: Joan Blondell. Garth: Lee J. Cobb. (90 min.)

10 DAYS OF OUR LIVES

12 VIRGINIAN
The Virginian struggles to turn an Eastern dandy into a Shiloh hand. Austin: Robert Pine. Morgan: Michael Masters. Virginian: James Drury. Elizabeth: Sara Lane. (90 min.)

3:45

2 CARTOON INSTRUCTION BW
Lesson: caricatures.

4:00

2 MISTER ROGERS
Making your own choices is a topic.

4 I LOVE LUCY BW
It's wives vs. husbands when Lucy and Ethel make a bet with Ricky and Fred over who will catch the biggest fish on a deep-sea fishing trip. Lucy: Lucille Ball.

6 HIGH CHAPARRAL
Kevin McCarthy and Jack Elam in a chilling episode with a desert stagecoach holdup, a struggle for survival and a plot to kill John Cannon (Leif Erickson). (60 min.)

10 DOCTORS

4:30

2 ELECTRIC COMPANY

4 PONDEROSA
Sullen young Billy Allen seems to be warming up to Hoss—until his father escapes from prison and Billy goes back into his hostile shell. Billy: David Ladd. Hoss: Dan Blocker. Pen: Lorne Greene. Adam: Pernell Roberts. Little Joe: Michael Landon. Vance Allen: Logan Field. Pike: Robert Tetrick. (60 min.)

7 GILLIGAN'S ISLAND

10 ANOTHER WORLD

11 MIKE DOUGLAS
Herbie Mann, Stiller and Meara, and psychologist Cylvia Sorkin are the guests. Joe Harnell sextet. (60 min.)

5:00

2 SESAME STREET

3 7 ABC NEWS—Howard K. Smith, Harry Reasoner

6 RIFLEMAN BW
A prowler is loose near the Seevers ranch, and Lucas remembers that Cora Seevers is home alone. Lucas: Chuck Connors. Cora: Patricia Breslin. Jason Gowdy: Richard Anderson.

8 I DREAM OF JEANNIE
Things get a bit sticky when Dr. Bellows (Hayden Rorke) discovers a strength-inducing candy concocted by Jeannie's mother. Jeannie/Mother: Barbara Eden.

10 TRUTH OR CONSEQUENCES

12 PETTICOAT JUNCTION
Betty Jo and Steve have their first lovers' quarrel over a ramshackle place Betty envisions as the house beautiful. Kate: Bea Benaderet. Betty Jo: Linda Kaye. Steve: Mike Minor. Uncle Joe: Edgar Buchanan.

5:30

3 NEWS

4 6 NBC NEWS—Chancellor

7 TRUTH OR CONSEQUENCES

8 11 12 CBS NEWS—Cronkite

10 ABC NEWS—Smith/Reasoner

DECEMBER 7, 1972

EVENING

6:00 **2** AMERICANS FROM AFRICA (BW)
Topic: "NAACP, Urban League and Early Battles for Rights."
3 TRUTH OR CONSEQUENCES
4 **6** **7** **8** **10** **11** **12** NEWS
6:30 **2** ARKANSAS GAME AND FISH (BW)
3 TO TELL THE TRUTH
4 FACEOFF—Len Day
6 DRAGNET
A lady writer on women's careers known for her hatchet jobs just might not glorify the role of a policewoman. Friday: Jack Webb. Dorothy Lee: Virginia Gregg. Gannon: Harry Morgan. Joyce Anderson: Susan Seaforth.
7 DRAGNET
8 EVIL TOUCH—Drama
Leslie Nielsen as the skipper of an old schooner that seems to be charting its own course. Craig Larsen: Terence Cooper. Pamela Larsen: Jill Forster.
10 REEL FUN
11 JERRY McKINNIS—Fishing
12 BUCK OWENS
7:00 **2** ADVOCATES
"Should you support the Lettuce Boycott?" Tonight's forum centers on the two-year strike by Cesar Chavez's United Farm Workers against California growers. Issues include the involvement of the Teamsters Union in the dispute. (60 min.)
3 **7** **10** MOD SQUAD
Is she accident prone—or a killer's target? The squad probes for the truth about ex-child star Belinda, the recent victim of several potentially lethal mishaps. Pete: Michael Cole. Linc: Clarence Williams III. (60 min.)
Guest Cast
Belinda ....Cathy Burns
Tony ....Robert Balaban
Irenee ....Ruth Roman
Blake Morris ....Dane Clark
Charley Ince ....Anthony James
4 **6** **8** FLIP WILSON
Tony Randall, Dionne Warwicke, and comics Burns and Schreiber are the guests. Comedy . . . Tony as a stuffy board chairman, a fast-talking DJ (plugging records of the Fifties), a staid bird-watcher and an acupunc-

Thursday
EVENING

turist giving Flip the needle. Burns and Schreiber do a routine about a psychiatrist and a puffy patient who thinks he's a balloon. (60 min.)
Highlights
"Day Dreaming," "Anyone Who Had a Heart" ....Dionne
11 **12** THE WALTONS—Drama
The plight of dust-bowl refugees is the core of a story about the Walton's visiting cousins from Kansas. John-Boy: Richard Thomas. John: Ralph Waite. Olivia: Michael Learned. Grandpa: Will Geer. Grandma: Ellen Corby. Mary Ellen: Judy Norton. Jason: Jon Walmsley. (60 min.)
Guest Cast
Ham Denby ....Warren Vanders
Cora Denby ....Jay MacIntosh
Job Denby ....Ken Wolger
8:00 **2** INTERNATIONAL PERFORMANCE
One of the important ballets of an era . . . "La Sylphide" ushered in the Romantic Age of the 19th century. The story follows a young Scottish nobleman who falls in love with a woodland sprite; she dies in his arms when captured. As one critic wrote of the style and the era . . . "it mirrored man's higher aspirations for beauty. The creatures of fantasy, almost always unobtainable, symbolized the dreams and hopes of man." (60 min.)
Cast
La Sylphide ..... Ghislaine Thesmar
James ....Michael Denard
Effie ....Laurence Nerval
3 **7** **10** ASSIGNMENT: VIENNA —Crime Drama
Rosemary Forsyth as a woman out of Jake's past, seeking aid in clearing her husband of a murder rap. Victor Buono has a juicy role as a baddie. Jake: Robert Conrad. Caldwell: Charles Cioffi. (60 min.)
Guest Cast
Annalisa ....Rosemary Forsyth
Karafatma ....Victor Buono
Jonathan ....John Ericson
Shelton ....Paul Mantee
Ibn Faris ....Abraham Sofaer
Klimenko ....Peter Herald
4 **6** IRONSIDE
Prostitutes and panders are Chief

Thursday
EVENING

Ironside's only source of help as he tries to solve a call girl's murder. Ironside: Raymond Burr. Fran: Elizbeth Baur. (60 min.)

Guest Cast
Wanda Bolen ....Tisha Sterling
Johnny Andrews ....John Quade
Lieutenant Reese .....Johnny Seven
Anton Bolen ....Titos Vandis

8 12 MOVIE—Adventure
Bogart and Hepburn in a 1951 classic: "The African Queen." Bogie shines in his Oscar-winning performance as a gin-guzzling river tramp sharing a perilous 1000-mile journey on uncharted rivers with a prim missionary lady (Hepburn). Directed in Africa by John Huston. (2 hrs., 10 min.)

Cast
Charlie Allnut ....Humphrey Bogart
Rose Sayer .....Katharine Hepburn
Samuel Sayer ....Robert Morley

11 MOVIE—Drama
"Lost Flight." (1970) Passengers on a downed air liner fight to survive on a tropical island. Lloyd Bridges, Anne Francis. Glenn: Ralph Meeker. Jonesy: Andrew Prine. Eddie: Bobby Van. Delaney: Michael Larrain. Barnaby: Billy Dee Williams. (2 hrs.)

9:00 2 WORLD PRESS
3 7 10 OWEN MARSHALL
Tab Hunter stars as a disc jockey who kills his wife and pins it on someone else; James Stacy plays the sportscaster caught in the frame. Marshall: Arthur Hill. Jess: Lee Majors. Frieda: Joan Darling. (60 min.)

Guest Cast
Howard Reimer ....Tab Hunter
Ray Scoby ....James Stacy
Assistant DA Escobedo
    ....Nate Esformes

4 6 DEAN MARTIN
Carol Channing and Mike "Mannix" Connors are the guests. Comedy: Carol and Dean in a sketch about a plant psychiatrist. Also: film clips from MGM's "Show Boat" (1951), featuring Howard Keel, Kathryn Grayson, Ava Gardner, Joe E. Brown, Marge and Gower Champion. Dom DeLuise, Nipsey Russell, Rodney Dangerfield, Kay Medford, the Ding-a-Lings. (60 min.)

Highlights
"On an Evening in Roma" ....Dean
"Brand New Key" ....Carol
"Almost Like Being in Love"
    .... Dean, Ding-a-Lings
"Show Boat" finale ....All
"Hands" ....Ding-a-Lings
"The Sun Is Shining," "I'm Always Chasing Rainbows"
    .... Dean, Ding-a-Lings

9:30 2 THIRTY MINUTES WITH
—Interview

10:00 2 WORLD PRESS
3 4 6 7 10 11 NEWS

10:10 8 12 NEWS

10:30 3 7 10 TRUMAN CAPOTE BEHIND PRISON WALLS
Special: "I have my own kind of justice" is the way one San Quentin prisoner explains his rationale for murder to Truman Capote. Violence, drugs, homosexuality and penal reform are discussed in Capote's recent interviews with convicts, an assistant warden and a guard. Taped in October 1972. (90 min.)

4 6 JOHNNY CARSON
Carol Burnett and singer Bobby Goldsboro are scheduled. (90 min.)

11 MOVIE—Comedy BW
"We're Not Married." (1952) Five couples learn that they are not legally married. Ramona: Ginger Rogers. Steve Gladwin: Fred Allen. Justice of the Peace: Victor Moore. Annabel Norris: Marilyn Monroe. Jeff Norris: David Wayne. Katie Woodruff: Eve Arden. Hector Woodruff: Paul Douglas. Willie Fisher: Eddie Bracken. Patsy Fisher: Mitzi Gaynor. Freddie Melrose: Louis Calhern. Eve Melrose: Zsa Zsa Gabor.

10:40 8 12 MOVIE—Drama
Sidney Poitier and Elizabeth Hartman in "A Patch of Blue," a poignant 1965 love story about two people who reach across the color barrier. Shelley Winters. (2 hrs., 10 min.)

12:00 3 7 10 SAN QUENTIN
—Discussion
Prison reform experts react to "Truman Capote Behind Prison Walls." The panel discussion is expected to deal with alternative penal systems. At press time, guests were not named.

12:50 8 NEWS

A-52 TV GUIDE